Contents

KU-532-298

Addison Wesley Longman Limited
Edinburgh Gate, Harlow,
Essex CM20 2JE, England
and Associated Companies throughout the world.

First published in the Longman Simplified English Series 1936
First published in Longman Fiction 1993
This edition first published in 1996

ISBN 0 582 27513 X

Set in Adobe Granjon 10.5pt
Printed in China

Acknowledgements

We are grateful to Addison Wesley Longman Limited for
permission to use in the Word List definitions adapted
from the third edition of the *Longman Dictionary of
Contemporary English* © Longman Group Limited (1995).

Cover photograph © Addison Wesley Longman Limited/Gareth Boden

Upper Intermediate level books in the Longman Fiction series are simplified with reference to the
Longman Defining Vocabulary.
Vocabulary level: 2000 words

Introduction

Herbert George Wells was born in 1866 in Bromley, England into a family where there was little money to spare; his father ran a small shop and played cricket professionally and his mother worked as a housekeeper. The family's financial situation meant that Wells had to work from the age of fourteen to support himself through education. His success at school won him a free place to study at a college of science in London, after which he became a science teacher. His poor health made life difficult, though, and he struggled to keep his full-time job while trying to write in his spare time.

He married twice. His first wife was Isabel Mary Wells, but the marriage was not a success. Three years later he left her for Amy Catherine Robbins, a former pupil. Wells often criticised the institution of marriage, and he had relationships with several other women, the most important being the writer Rebecca West. By 1895 Wells had become a full-time writer and lived comfortably from his work. He travelled a lot and kept homes in the south of France and in London, where he died in 1946.

Wells wrote about forty works of fiction and collections of stories; many books and shorter works on political, social and historical matters; three books for children, and one about his own life. His most important early works established him as the father of science fiction and it is for these books that he is remembered. Best known are *The Time Machine* (1895), *The Invisible Man* (1897), *The War of the Worlds* (1898) and *The First Men in the Moon* (1901). In all these works he shows a remarkable imagination and a gift for making the impossible seem possible. He seemed to have the ability to make intelligent guesses about future scientific developments; he described travel underwater and by air, for example, at a time when such journeys seemed to be pure fiction.

Wells began to realise that his science fiction, although highly successful, was not about the lives of real people, and the subject matter of his later works of fiction is rooted in a world of which he had personal experience. *Love and Mr Lewisham* (1900) tells the story of a struggling teacher. *The History of Mr Polly* (1910) describes the adventures of a shopkeeper who frees himself from his work by burning down his own shop and running away to start a new life. In these and other books he shows a sympathetic interest in, and understanding for, the lives of ordinary people that were rarely present in fiction at the time. One of Wells's most successful works is *Tono-Bungay* (1909), a story of dishonesty and greed involving the production and sale of a medicine that, for a time, brings wealth and respect to its inventor.

For centuries storytellers have been interested in the idea of invisible beings, with all the related possibilities and dangers. Wells's interest in the subject is from a scientific rather than a magical point of view, and he uses the main character in *The Invisible Man* to put across his message that scientific progress can be dangerous in the wrong hands. Apart from the idea of invisibility, the rest of the book is very realistic. It is set in a real place known to Wells; the characters are ordinary and believable. All of this makes the less believable central idea easier to accept. Much of the book is written with a light, humorous touch, but it becomes more serious as the story develops.

The story begins on a snowy winter's day in the village of Iping. A mysterious stranger arrives at the Coach and Horses Inn, wrapped up from head to foot so that no part of his body is visible. The lady of the inn, Mrs Hall, is pleased to have a guest at this time of year, but her pleasure turns to doubt and finally to fear as she discovers her strange visitor's secret. When he begins to make trips out of the inn, the people of the village and surrounding area are affected by the appearance and behaviour of the Invisible Man and they connect his presence with robberies and strange events in the area. It is the scientist, Dr Kemp, who the Invisible Man turns to for help and understanding, and who learns the secret of the strange man's invisibility. When the Invisible Man finds that he was wrong to have trusted Kemp, his actions become wilder and more violent and it is clear that the story will not end happily.

Chapter 1

The Strange Man's Arrival

The stranger came early one winter's day in February, through a biting wind and the last snowfall of the year. He walked over the hill from Bramblehurst Station, and carried a little black bag in his thickly gloved hand. He was wrapped up from head to foot, and the edge of his soft grey hat hid every part of his face except the shiny point of his nose; the snow had piled itself against his shoulders and chest. He almost fell into the Coach and Horses, more dead than alive, and threw his bag down. "A fire," he cried, "in the name of human kindness! A room and a fire!" He stamped his feet, shook the snow from his coat and followed Mrs Hall, the innkeeper's wife, into her parlour. There he arranged to take a room in the inn and gave her two pounds.

Mrs Hall lit the fire and left him there while she went to prepare him a meal with her own hands. To have a guest at Iping in the winter time was an unusual piece of good fortune, and she was determined to show that she deserved it.

She put some meat on the fire to cook, told Millie, the servant, to get the room ready for the stranger, and carried the cloth, plates and glasses into the parlour, and began to lay the table. Although the fire was burning brightly, she was surprised to see that her visitor still wore his hat and coat, and stood with his back to her, looking out of the window at the falling snow in the yard.

His gloved hands were held behind him, and he seemed to be thinking deeply. She noticed that some melted snow was falling onto the floor from his shoulders.

"Can I take your hat and coat, sir," she said, "and dry them in the kitchen?"

"No," he replied, without turning.

She was not sure that she had heard him, and was about to repeat the question.

He turned his head and looked at her over his shoulder. "I would rather keep them on," he said firmly; and she noticed that he wore big blue glasses, and had a bushy beard over his coat collar that almost hid his face.

"Very well, sir," she said. "As you like. Very soon the room will be warmer."

He made no answer, and turned his face away from her again, and Mrs Hall, feeling that her talk was unwelcome, finished laying the table quickly, and hurried out of the room. When she returned he was still standing there like a man of stone, his collar turned up, the edge of his hat turned down, almost hiding his face and ears. She put down the eggs and meat noisily, and called rather than said to him:

"Your lunch is served, sir."

"Thank you," he answered. He did not move until she was closing the door. Then he turned round and walked eagerly up to the table.

Mrs Hall filled the butter dish in the kitchen, and took it to the parlour.

She knocked and entered at once. As she did so her visitor moved quickly, so that she only saw something white disappearing behind the table. He seemed to be picking up something from the floor. She put down the butter dish on the table, and noticed that the visitor's hat and coat were hanging over a chair in front of the fire.

"I suppose I may have them to dry now?" she said, in a voice that could not be refused.

"Leave the hat," said her visitor, and turning, she saw he had raised his head and was looking at her.

For a moment she stood looking at him, too surprised to speak.

He held his napkin over the lower part of his face, so that his mouth and jaws were completely hidden. But it was not that which surprised

Mrs Hall. It was the fact that the top of his head above his blue glasses was covered by a white bandage, and that another covered his ears, leaving nothing of his face to be seen except his pink, pointed nose. It was bright pink, and shining, just as it had been at first. He wore a dark brown jacket, with a high black collar turned up about his neck. His thick black hair stuck out below and between the bandages. This bandaged head was so unlike what she had expected that for a moment she stood staring at it.

He did not remove the napkin, but remained holding it, as she saw now, with a brown-gloved hand, and looking at her from behind his dark glasses.

"Leave the hat," he said, through the white cloth.

She began to feel less afraid. She put the hat on the chair again by the fire.

"I didn't know, sir," she began, "that——" And she stopped.

"Thank you," he said shortly, looking from her to the door, and then at her again.

"I'll have it nicely dried, sir, at once," she said, and carried his coat out of the room. She looked at his bandaged head and dark glasses again as she was going out of the door; but he was still holding his napkin in front of his face. She was shaking a little as she closed the door behind her. "My goodness!" she whispered. She went straight to the kitchen, and did not even think of asking Millie what she was doing now.

The visitor sat and listened to her footsteps. He looked out of the window before he removed his napkin from his face and began his meal again. He took a mouthful, looked again at the window, took another mouthful; then rose and, taking the napkin in his hand, walked across the room and pulled down the blind. This darkened the room. He returned more happily to the table and his meal.

"The poor man's had an accident, or an operation or something," said Mrs Hall. "What a shock those bandages gave me."

She put some more coal on the fire, and hung the traveller's coat to dry. "And the glasses! Why, he doesn't look human at all. And holding that napkin over his mouth all the time. Talking through it! . . . Perhaps his mouth was hurt too."

She turned round, suddenly remembering something. "Oh dear!" she said, "Haven't you done those potatoes yet, Millie?"

When Mrs Hall went to clear away the stranger's lunch, her idea that his mouth must also have been damaged in an accident was strengthened, for though he was smoking a pipe, all the time that she was in the room he kept the lower part of his face covered. He sat in the corner with his back to the window, and spoke now, having eaten and drunk and being comfortably warmed through, less impatiently than before. The light of the fire shone red in his glasses.

"I have some boxes," he said, "at Bramblehurst Station. How can they be brought here?"

Mrs Hall answered his question, and then said, "It's a steep road by the hill, sir. That's where a carriage was turned over, a year ago and more. A gentleman was killed. Accidents, sir, happen in a moment, don't they?"

"They do."

"But people take long enough to get well, sir, don't they? There was my sister's son, Tom, who cut his arm with a scythe — he fell on it out in the fields. He was three months tied up, sir. You'd hardly believe it. I've been afraid of scythes ever since, sir."

"I can quite understand that," said the visitor.

"We were afraid that he'd have to have an operation, he was so bad, sir."

The visitor laughed suddenly.

"Was he?"

"He was, sir. And it wasn't funny for those who had to nurse him as I did, my sister being so busy with her little ones. There were bandages to do, sir, and bandages to undo. So that if I may say, sir——"

"Will you get me some matches?" said the visitor quite suddenly. "My pipe is out."

Mrs Hall stopped. It was certainly rude of him after she had told him so much. But she remembered the two pounds, and went for the matches.

"Thanks," he said shortly, as she put them down, and turned his back upon her and looked out of the window again. Clearly he did not like talking about bandages.

The visitor remained in the room until four o'clock, without giving Mrs Hall an excuse for a visit. He was very quiet during that time: perhaps he sat in the growing darkness smoking by the firelight — perhaps he slept.

Once or twice a listener might have heard him: for five minutes he could be heard walking up and down the room. He seemed to be talking to himself. Then he sat down again in the armchair.

Chapter 2

Mr Henfrey Has a Shock

At four o'clock, when it was fairly dark, and Mrs Hall was trying to find the courage to go in and ask her visitor if he would like some tea, Teddy Henfrey, the clock-mender, came into the bar.

"Good evening, Mrs Hall," said he, "this is terrible snowy weather for thin boots!"

Mrs Hall agreed, and then noticed he had his bag with him. "Now you're here, Mr Teddy," said she, "I'd be glad if you'd look at the old clock. It's going, and it strikes loud and clear, but the hour hand does nothing except point to six."

And, leading the way, she went across to the parlour door and knocked.

As she opened the door, she saw her visitor seated in the armchair in front of the fire, asleep, it seemed, with his bandaged head leaning on one side. The only light in the room was from the fire. Everything seemed hidden in shadows. But for a second it seemed to her that the man she was looking at had a great, wide-open mouth, a mouth that swallowed the whole of the lower part of his face. It was too ugly to believe, the white head, the staring glasses — and then a great hole. He moved, sat up straight and put up his hand. She opened the door wide, so that the room was lighter, and she saw him more clearly, with the napkin held to his face, just as she had seen him hold it before. The shadows, she thought, had tricked her.

"Would you mind, sir, if this man came to look at the clock, sir?" she said.

"Look at the clock?" he said, staring round sleepily and speaking over his hand; and then, more fully awake, "Certainly."

Mrs Hall went away to get a lamp, and he rose and stretched himself. Then came the light, and at the door Mr Teddy Henfrey was met by this bandaged person. He was, he said later, "quite shocked".

"Good afternoon," said the stranger, staring at him — as Mr Henfrey said — "like a fish".

"I hope," said Mr Henfrey, "that you don't mind."

"Not at all," said the stranger. "Though I understood," he said, turning to Mrs Hall, "that this room was to be mine for my own use."

"I thought, sir," said Mrs Hall, "you'd like the clock——"

"Certainly," said the stranger, "certainly; but at other times I would like to be left alone."

He turned round with his back to the fireplace, and put his hands behind his back. "And soon," he said, "when the clock is mended, I think

I should like to have some tea. But not until then."

Mrs Hall was about to leave the room — she did not try to talk this time — when her visitor asked her if she had done anything about his boxes at Bramblehurst. She told him that the carrier could bring them over the next day.

"You are certain that is the earliest?" he asked. She was quite sure.

"I should explain," he added, "but I was really too cold and tired to do so before, that I am a scientist."

"Indeed, sir," said Mrs Hall, respectfully.

"And I need things from the boxes for my work."

"Of course, sir."

"My reason for coming to Iping," he went on slowly, "was a desire to be alone. I do not wish to be disturbed in my work. Besides my work, an accident——"

"I thought so," said Mrs Hall to herself.

"——makes it necessary for me to be quiet. My eyes are sometimes so weak and painful that I have to shut myself up in the dark for several hours and lock myself in. Sometimes — now and then. Not at present, certainly. At such times the least thing, even a stranger coming into the room, gives me great pain. It's important that this should be understood."

"Certainly, sir," said Mrs Hall. "And if I might ask——"

"That, I think, is all," said the stranger quietly.

Mrs Hall said no more.

After Mrs Hall had left the room, he remained standing in front of the fire and watched the clock being mended. Mr Henfrey worked with the lamp close to him, and the green shade threw a bright light onto his hands and onto the frame and wheels, and left the rest of the room in shadow. He took longer than he needed to remove the works, hoping to have some talk with the stranger. But the stranger stood there, perfectly silent and still. So still that it frightened Henfrey. He felt alone in the room and looked up, and there, grey and shadowy, were the bandaged head and large dark glasses staring straight in front of them. It was so strange to Henfrey that for a minute they stood staring at each other. Then Henfrey looked down again. He would have liked to say something. Should he say that the weather was very cold for the time of the year?

"The weather——" he began.

"Why don't you finish and go?" said the stiff figure, angrily. "All you've got to do is to fix the hour hand. You're simply wasting time."

"Certainly, sir — one minute more. I forgot . . ." And Mr Henfrey finished and left the room.

"Really!" said Mr Henfrey to himself, walking down the village street through the falling snow. "A man must mend a clock sometimes, surely." And then, "Can't a man look at you? Ugly!"

And yet again, "It seems he can't. If you were wanted by the police, you couldn't be more wrapped and bandaged."

At the street corner he saw Hall, who had recently married the lady of the inn. "Hello, Teddy," said Hall, as he passed.

"You've got a strange visitor!" said Teddy.

Hall stopped. "What did you say?" he asked.

"A strange man is staying at the inn," said Teddy. And he described Mrs Hall's guest. "It looks strange, doesn't it? I'd like to see a man's face if I had him staying in my house. But women are so foolish with strangers. He's taken your rooms, and he hasn't even given a name."

"Is that so?" said Hall, rather stupidly.

"Yes," said Teddy. "And he's got a lot of boxes coming tomorrow, so he says."

Teddy walked on, easier in his mind.

And after the stranger had gone to bed, which he did at about half past nine, Mr Hall went into the parlour and looked very hard at the furniture, just to show that the stranger wasn't master there. When he went to bed, he told Mrs Hall to look very closely at the stranger's boxes when they came next day.

"You mind your own business, Hall," said Mrs Hall, "and I'll mind mine."

But in the middle of the night she woke up dreaming of great white heads that came after her, at the end of long necks, and with big black eyes. But being a sensible woman, she turned over and went to sleep again.

Chapter 3

The Thousand and One Bottles

That was how, on the ninth day of February, the stranger came to Iping village. Next day his boxes arrived. There were two trunks, indeed, such as any man might have, but also there was a box of books — big, fat books, of which some were in handwriting you couldn't read — and twelve or more boxes and cases full of glass bottles, or so it seemed to Hall, as he pulled at the paper packing material. The stranger, covered up in hat, coat and gloves, came out impatiently to meet the carriage, while Hall was talking to Fearenside, the carrier, before helping to bring the boxes in. The stranger did not notice Fearenside's dog, who was smelling at Hall's legs.

"Come along with those boxes," he said. "I've been waiting long enough." And he came down the steps, as if to pick up the smaller case.

As soon as Fearenside's dog caught sight of him, however, it began to growl, and when he ran down the steps it went straight for his hand. Hall cried out and jumped back, for he was not very brave with dogs, and

Fearenside shouted, "Lie down!" and reached for his whip.

They saw that the dog's teeth had missed the stranger's hand, heard a kick, saw the dog jump and bite the stranger's leg, and heard the sound of his trousers tearing. Then Fearenside's whip cut into his dog, who, crying with pain, ran under the wheels of the carriage. It was all done in a quick half minute. No one spoke, everyone shouted. The stranger looked at his torn glove and at his leg, then turned and ran up the steps into the inn. They heard him go across the passage and up the stairs to his bedroom.

"Come here, you!" said Fearenside to his dog, climbing off the carriage with his whip in his hand, while the dog watched him through the wheel. "Come here!" he repeated. "You'd better!"

Hall stood staring. "He was bitten," he said. "I'd better go and see him." And he went to find the stranger. He met his wife in the passage. "The carrier's dog bit him," he told her.

He went straight upstairs, pushed open the stranger's door and went in.

The blind was down and the room dark. He caught sight of a strange thing, a handless arm that seemed to be waving towards him, and a face of three large dark spots on white. Then he was struck in the chest and thrown out of the room, and the door was shut in his face and locked. All this happened so fast that it gave him no time to see anything clearly. A waving of shapes, a blow and a noise like a gun. There he stood in the dark little passage, wondering what he had seen.

After a few minutes he came back to the little group that had formed outside the inn. There was Fearenside telling the story all over again for the second time; there was Mrs Hall saying his dog had no right to bite her guests; there was Huxter, the shopkeeper from over the road, asking questions; Sandy Wadgers looking serious and women and children, all talking.

Mr Hall, staring at them from the steps and listening, found it hard to believe that he had seen anything very strange happen upstairs.

"He wants no help, he says," he said in answer to his wife's question. "We'd better take his luggage in."

"He ought to have his leg looked at immediately," said Mr Huxter.

"I'd shoot the dog, that's what I'd do," said a lady in the group.

Suddenly the dog began growling again.

"Come along," cried an angry voice in the doorway, and there stood the stranger, with his coat collar turned up and the edge of his hat bent down.

"The sooner you get those things in, the better I'll be pleased." His trousers and gloves had been changed.

"Were you hurt, sir?" said Fearenside. "I'm very sorry the dog——"

"Not at all," said the stranger. "It didn't even break the skin. Hurry up with those things."

As soon as the first box was carried into the parlour, the stranger began to unpack it eagerly, and from it he brought out bottles — little fat bottles, small thin bottles, blue bottles, bottles with round bodies and thin necks, large green glass bottles, large white glass bottles, wine bottles, bottles, bottles, bottles — and put them in rows on the table under the window, round the floor, on the shelf — everywhere. Case after case was full of bottles; he emptied six of the cases and piled the packing material high on the floor and table.

As soon as the cases were empty, the stranger went to the window and set to work, not troubling in the least about the paper, the fire which had gone out, the box of books outside or the boxes and other things that had gone upstairs.

When Mrs Hall took his dinner in to him, he did not hear her until she had cleared away most of the paper and had put the food on the table. Then he half turned his head, and turned it away again. But she saw he had taken off his glasses; they were beside him on the table, and he seemed to her to have no eyes. He put on his glasses again, and then turned and faced her. She was about to complain about the paper on the floor, but he spoke first.

"I wish you wouldn't come in without knocking," he said, angrily as usual.

"I knocked, but——"

"But in my work I cannot have any — I must ask you——"

"Certainly, sir. You can turn the key if you want to, you know. Any time."

"A very good idea," said the stranger.

"This paper, sir. If I might say——"

"Don't. If the paper is a problem, put it on the bill."

He was so strange, standing there, with his bottles and his bad temper, that Mrs Hall was quite afraid. But she was a strong-minded woman. "Then I should like to know, sir, what you consider——"

"A shilling — put a shilling on my bill. Surely a shilling's enough?"

"Very well," said Mrs Hall, taking up the tablecloth and beginning to spread it over the table.

"If you're satisfied, of course——"

He turned his back on her and sat down.

All afternoon he worked with the door locked, and almost in silence. But once there was a noise of bottles ringing together, as though the table had been hit, and the crash of glass thrown down, and then came the sound of quick walking up and down the room. Fearing something was the matter, she went to the door and listened, not wanting to knock.

"I can't go on," he was shouting; "I *can't* go on! Three hundred thousand, four hundred thousand! It may take me all my life! . . . Patience! Patience, indeed! . . . Fool! Fool!"

There was a noise of boots on the brick floor of the bar, and Mrs Hall could not stay to hear any more. When she returned, the room was silent again except for the faint sound of his chair and now and then of a bottle.

It was all over; the stranger had returned to his work.

Later, when she took in his tea, she saw broken glass in the corner of the room. She pointed at it.

"Put it on the bill," he said. "In God's name don't worry me! If there's damage done, put it on the bill." And he went on with his writing.

"I'll tell you something," said Fearenside. It was late in the afternoon, and they were in a little inn outside Iping.

"Well?" said Teddy Henfrey.

"This man you're speaking of, that my dog bit. Well — he's black. At least his legs are. I saw through the tear in his trousers and the tear in his glove. You'd have expected a sort of pink to show, wouldn't you? Well — there was just blackness. I tell you he's as black as my hat."

"Good heavens!" said Henfrey. "It's a very strange case indeed. Why, his nose is as pink as paint!"

"That's true," said Fearenside. "I know that. And I tell you what I'm thinking. That man's black here and white there — in pieces. And he daren't show it. He's a kind of half-breed. I've heard of such things before. And it's common with horses, as anyone can see."

Chapter 4

Mr Cuss Talks to the Stranger

The stranger rarely left the inn by day, but in the evening he would go out, wrapped up to the eyes, whether the weather was cold or not, and he chose the loneliest paths. His glasses and bandaged face under his great black hat would appear suddenly out of the darkness to one or two workmen going home, and one night Teddy Henfrey, coming out of the

Dog and Duck, was frightened by the stranger's white, round head (he was walking hat in hand) lit by the sudden light of the open inn door. It seemed doubtful whether the stranger hated boys more than they hated him, but there was certainly hatred enough on both sides.

Of course they talked about him in Iping, and were unable to decide what his business was. Mrs Hall said he "discovered things", that he had had an accident, and that he did not like people to see the ugly marks on his body. Some said that he was a criminal hiding from the police, and others that he was part white and part black, and "if he chose to show himself at fairs he would make a great deal of money". A few thought that he was simply and harmlessly mad. And in the end some of the women began to think that he was a spirit or a magician.

No one liked him, for he was always angry and never friendly. They drew to one side as he passed down the village street, and when he had gone by young men would put their coat collars up and turn the edges of their hats down, and follow him for a joke.

Cuss, the doctor, was interested in the bandages and bottles. All through April and May he wanted to talk to the stranger, and at last he could bear it no longer and went to visit him. He was surprised to find that Mr Hall did not know his guest's name.

"He gave a name," said Mrs Hall — this was untrue — "but I didn't hear it properly." She thought it seemed silly not to know the man's name.

Cuss could hear swearing inside the parlour. He knocked at the door and entered.

"Please forgive me for breaking in on you," said Cuss, and then the door closed and shut out Mrs Hall.

She could hear the sound of voices for the next ten minutes, then a cry of surprise, a moving of feet, a chair being knocked over, a laugh, quick steps to the door, and Cuss appeared, his face white, his eyes staring over his shoulder. He left the door open behind him and, without looking at her, went across the hall and down the steps, and she heard his feet hurrying along the road. He carried his hat in his hand. She stood behind the bar, looking at the open door of the parlour. Then she heard the stranger laughing quietly, and his footsteps came across the room. She could not see his face from where she stood. The parlour door shut loudly, and the place was silent again.

Cuss went straight up the village to Bunting, the vicar.

"Am I mad?" Cuss began, as he entered the little study. "Do I look like a madman?"

"What's happened?" asked the vicar.

"That man at the inn . . ."

"Well?"

"Give me something to drink," said Cuss, and he sat down.

When his nerves had been steadied by a glass of wine he said, "As I went in, he put his hands in his pockets and then he sat down in his chair. I told him I'd heard he took an interest in scientific things. He said, 'Yes.' I tried to talk to him. He got quite angry . . . Well, he told me that he had had a piece of paper. It was important, most important, most valuable. A list of . . . 'Was it medicine?' I asked. 'Why do you want to know?' was his answer. In any case, this paper was of great value. He had read it, put it down on the table and looked away. Then the wind had lifted it and blown it into the fire. He saw it go up the chimney. Just as he told me that, he lifted his arm. The sleeve was empty. I could see right up it. What can keep a sleeve up and open if there's nothing in it?

" 'How can you move an empty sleeve like that?' I asked.

" 'Empty sleeve?' he said.

" 'Yes,' I said, 'an empty sleeve.'

" 'It's an empty sleeve, is it? You saw it was an empty sleeve?' He stood up. I stood up too. He came towards me in three very slow steps, and stood quite close.

" 'You said it was an empty sleeve?' he said.

" 'Certainly,' I said.

"Then very quietly he pulled his sleeve out of his pocket again, and raised his arm towards me, as though he would show it to me again. He did it very, very slowly. I looked at it, holding my breath. 'Well?' I said, clearing my throat; 'there's nothing in it.'

"I was beginning to feel frightened. I could see right down it. He put it out straight towards me, slowly, slowly — just like that — until it was six inches from my face. Just imagine seeing an empty sleeve come at you like that! And then——"

"Well?"

"Something — it felt exactly like a finger and a thumb — pulled my nose."

Bunting began to laugh.

"There wasn't anything there!" said Cuss, his voice rising to a shout at the "there". "You may laugh if you like, but I tell you I was so shocked that I hit his sleeve hard and turned round and ran out of the room I left him——"

Cuss stopped. It was easy to see that he was afraid. He turned round in a helpless way, and took a second glass of wine. "When I hit his sleeve," he said, "I tell you, it felt exactly like hitting an arm. And there wasn't an arm! There wasn't any arm at all!"

Mr Bunting thought it over. "It's a very strange story," he said. He looked very serious. "It really is a very strange story indeed."

Chapter 5

The Robbery at the Vicarage

The robbery at the Vicarage happened in the early hours of Whit Monday,* the day when Iping held its spring fair. Mrs Bunting, it seems, woke up suddenly in the stillness that comes before the sunrise, with a strong feeling that the door of their bedroom had opened and closed. She did not wake her husband at first, but sat up in bed listening. She then clearly heard the sound of bare feet coming out of the next room and walking along the passage towards the stairs. As soon as she felt sure of this, she woke her husband as quietly as she could. He did not light the lamp, but put on his glasses and a pair of soft shoes, and went out of the bedroom to listen. He heard quite clearly someone moving in the study downstairs, and then the sound of a violent sneeze.

At that he returned to his bedroom, armed himself with the poker, and went downstairs as silently as he could. Mrs Bunting stood at the top of the stairs.

It was about four o'clock, and the last darkness of the night had passed. There was a faint light in the passage; the study door stood half open. Everything was quiet and still, except the sound of the stairs under Mr Bunting's feet, and the slight movements in the study. He heard a drawer being opened, and a sound of papers. Then came some swearing, and a match was struck, and the study was full of yellow light. Mr Bunting was now in the hall, and through the half-open door he could see the desk, an open drawer, and a lamp burning on the desk. But he could not see the thief. He stood there considering what to do, and Mrs Bunting, her face white with fear, walked slowly downstairs after him.

* Whit Monday: the day after Whit Sunday (or Whitsun), which is an important day of celebration for Christians and falls on the seventh Sunday after Easter

They heard the noise of coins, and knew that the thief had found the housekeeping money — two pounds and ten shillings in gold and silver. That sound made Mr Bunting very angry. Holding the poker firmly, he ran into the room, closely followed by Mrs Bunting.

"Come on, my dear," and then Mr Bunting stopped. The room was perfectly empty.

But they knew that they had heard someone moving in the room. They stood still for half a minute. Then Mrs Bunting went across the room and looked behind the curtain, while Mr Bunting looked under the desk and up the chimney, and pushed the poker up into the darkness. Then they stood still looking at each other questioningly.

"I was quite sure——" said Mrs Bunting.

"The lamp!" said Mr Bunting. "Who lit the lamp?"

"The drawer!" said Mrs Bunting. "And the money's gone!"

She went quickly to the doorway.

"Who in the world——"

There was a loud sneeze in the passage. They rushed out, and as they did so the kitchen door closed!

"Bring the lamp!" said Mr Bunting, and led the way.

As he opened the kitchen door, he saw the back door opening. The garden beyond was lit by the first, faint light of sunrise. He was certain that nothing went out of the door. It stood open for a moment, and then closed with a loud bang. They searched outside for a minute or more before they came back into the kitchen.

The place was empty. They locked the back door and examined the kitchen and all the rooms thoroughly. There was no one to be found in the house, though they searched upstairs and down.

When daylight came, the vicar and his wife were still searching by the unnecessary light of the dying lamp.

"Of all the surprising events, this is——" began the vicar for the twentieth time.

"My dear," said Mrs Bunting, "there's the servant coming down. Just wait here until she has gone into the kitchen, and then go upstairs."

Chapter 6

The Furniture That Went Mad

When Mr Hall came downstairs in the early hours of Whit Monday, he noticed that the stranger's door was open and the front door unlocked. He remembered holding the lamp while Mrs Hall locked it the night before. At the sight of the front door he stopped; then he went upstairs again. He knocked at the stranger's door. There was no answer. He knocked again; then pushed the door wide open and entered.

It was as he expected. The bed, the room too, was empty. And what was still more strange, on the bed and chair were scattered the clothes, the only clothes so far as he knew, and the bandages of their guest. His big hat was hanging on the bedpost.

As Mr Hall stood there he heard his wife's voice coming from the kitchen.

He turned and hurried down to her.

"Jenny," he said, "he's not in his room and the front door is unlocked."

At first Mrs Hall did not understand, but as soon as she did she determined to see the empty room for herself. Hall went first. "If he's not there, his clothes are. And what is he doing without his clothes?"

As they came out of the kitchen they both thought they heard the front door open and shut but, seeing it closed and seeing nothing there, neither said a word to the other about it at the time. Mrs Hall passed her husband in the passage, and ran on first upstairs. Someone on the staircase sneezed. Mr Hall, following six steps behind, thought that he heard her sneeze; she, going first, thought that *he* was sneezing. She threw open the door and stood looking round the room. "What a strange thing!" she said.

She heard a cough close behind her, as it seemed, and, turning, was surprised to see her husband some distance away on the top stair. But in another moment he was beside her. She put her hand under the bedcovers.

"Cold," she said. "He's been up an hour or more."

At that point, a most unexpected thing happened. The bedcovers pulled themselves together into a pile, and then jumped violently off the bed. It was just as if a hand had thrown them to one side. Then the stranger's hat jumped off the bedpost, flew through the air, and came straight at Mrs Hall's face. Next, a piece of soap flew from the washstand. Finally the chair threw the stranger's coat and trousers carelessly onto the floor, laughed in a voice very like the stranger's, turned itself round so that its four legs pointed at Mrs Hall, seemed to take aim at her for a moment, and then moved quickly towards her. She cried out and turned, and the chair legs landed gently but firmly against her back and pushed her and Mr Hall out of the room. The door shut loudly and was locked. The chair and the bed seemed to be dancing for a moment, and then suddenly everything was still.

Mrs Hall was left almost fainting in Mr Hall's arms in the passage. It was with the greatest difficulty that Mr Hall and Millie, now dressed, succeeded in getting her downstairs.

"Spirits," said Mrs Hall. "I know it's spirits. I've read about them in the papers. Tables and chairs dancing."

"Lock him out," she went on. "Don't let him come in again. I half guessed . . . I might have known. With those eyes and that bandaged head, and never going to church on Sunday. And all those bottles — more than it's right for anyone to have. He's put the spirits into the furniture . . . My good old furniture! My poor dear mother used to sit in that chair when I was a little girl. And now it rises against me!"

They sent Millie across the street through the golden five o'clock sunshine to wake up Mr Sandy Wadgers, who was clever and might be able to help them.

"Magic," said Mr Wadgers and came to the inn greatly troubled. They wanted him to lead the way upstairs to the room, but he didn't seem to be in any hurry. He preferred to talk in the passage. Then Mr Huxter came and joined in the talk. There was a great deal of talking, but nothing was done.

"Let's have the facts first," said Mr Sandy Wadgers. "Let's be sure we'd be acting perfectly right in breaking that door open."

And suddenly the door of the room upstairs opened by itself, and they saw coming down the stairs the wrapped-up figure of the stranger staring more blackly than ever through those large glasses. He came down stiffly and slowly, staring all the time; he walked across the passage, staring, and then stopped.

He entered the parlour, and suddenly and angrily shut the door in their faces.

Not a word was spoken until the noise of the door had died away. They looked at one another.

"Well, I've never seen anything like it!" said Mr Wadgers, more troubled than ever.

"If I were you, I'd go in and ask him about it," Mr Wadgers advised Mr Hall. "I'd demand an explanation."

It took some time to persuade Mr Hall to do it. At last he knocked, opened the door, and got as far as:

"Excuse me——"

"Go to the devil!" said the stranger, "and shut that door after you."

And that was all.

Chapter 7

The Stranger Shows His Face

It was half past five when the stranger went into the little parlour of the Coach and Horses, and there he remained until nearly midday, with the blinds down and the door shut, and nobody went near him.

All that time he could have eaten nothing. Three times he rang his bell, the third time loud and long, but no one answered him. "Telling us to go to the devil, indeed!" said Mrs Hall. Soon came the story of the robbery at the Vicarage, and that started them thinking. Hall went off with Wadgers to find Mr Shuckleforth, the lawyer, and take his advice. No one went upstairs, and no one knew what the stranger was doing. Now and then he walked rapidly up and down, and they heard him swearing, tearing paper, breaking bottles.

The little group grew bigger. Mrs Huxter came over; some young fellows joined them. There was a stream of unanswered questions. Young Archie Harker tried to look under the closed curtains. He could see nothing, but he was soon joined by other boys.

And inside in the darkness of the parlour, the stranger, hungry and afraid, hidden in his uncomfortable hot clothes, stared through his dark glasses at his paper, or shook his dirty little bottles or swore at the boys outside the windows. In the corner by the fireplace lay the pieces of several broken bottles, and the sharp smell of a strange gas filled the air.

At about midday he suddenly opened his parlour door and stood looking at the three or four people in the bar. "Mrs Hall," he said. Somebody went and called for her.

She soon appeared, a little short of breath, and so even more angry. Hall was still out. She had had time to think now, and had brought the stranger's unpaid bill.

"Why wasn't my breakfast laid?" he asked. "Why haven't you prepared my meals and answered my bell? Do you think I can live without eating?"

"Why isn't my bill paid?" said Mrs Hall. "That's what I want to know."

"I told you three days ago I was expecting some money——"

"I told you three days ago I wasn't going to wait. You can't complain if your breakfast waits a bit, when my bill's been waiting for five days, can you?"

The stranger swore in answer.

"And I'd thank you, sir, if you'd keep your swearing to yourself, sir," said Mrs Hall.

"Look here, my good woman——" he began.

"Don't call me your good woman," said Mrs Hall.

"I've told you my money hasn't come."

"Money, indeed!" said Mrs Hall.

"Still, in my pocket——"

"You told me three days ago that you hadn't anything but a pound's worth of silver on you."

"Well, I've found some more."

"And where did you find that?" said Mrs Hall.

He stamped his foot. "What do you mean?" he said.

"I mean where did you find it?" said Mrs Hall. "And before I take any money, or get any breakfasts, or do any such things, you must tell me one or two things that I don't understand, and that nobody understands, and that everybody is very anxious to understand. I want to know what you have been doing to my chair upstairs, and I want to know why you went out of your bedroom and how you got in again. Those who stay here come in by the doors — that's the rule of this house, and *you* didn't do that, and what I want to know is how you *did* come in. And I want to know——"

Suddenly the stranger raised his gloved hands, stamped his foot, and said "Stop!" so loudly that he silenced her at once.

"You don't understand," he said, "who I am or what I am. I'll show you. By heaven! I'll show you." He put his open hand over his face and then took it away. His face became a black hole. "Here," he said. He stepped forward and handed Mrs Hall something which she, staring at his face, took without thinking. Then, when she saw what it was, she screamed loudly and dropped it. The nose — it was the stranger's nose, pink and shining! — rolled on the floor.

Then he removed his glasses, and everyone in the bar breathed deeply. He took off his hat, and tore at his beard and bandages.

It was worse than anything they had ever seen. Mrs Hall, open-mouthed with terror, ran to the door of the house.

Everyone began to move. They had expected burns, wounds, something ugly, but they saw — *nothing*! The bandages and false hair flew across the passage into the bar. Everyone fell over everyone else down the steps. For the man who stood there shouting was a man up to the shoulders, and then — *nothing*!

People down in the village heard shouts and saw the people rushing out of the inn. They saw Mrs Hall fall down, and Mr Henfrey jump, so as not to fall over her, and then they heard the frightful cries of Millie, who, running quickly from the kitchen at the noise, had come on the headless stranger from behind. Then her cries stopped suddenly.

Everyone in the village street, old and young, about forty or more of them, collected in a crowd around the inn door.

"What was he doing?"

"Ran at them with a knife."

"I heard the girl."

"No head, I tell you."

"Nonsense."

"Took off his bandages."

Everyone spoke at once. Suddenly Mr Hall appeared, very red and determined, then Mr Bobby Jaffers, the village policeman, and then the serious Mr Wadgers.

Mr Hall marched up the steps, walked straight to the door of the parlour and found it open.

"Policeman," he said, "do your duty."

Jaffers marched in, Hall next, Wadgers last. They saw the headless figure facing them, with a half-eaten piece of bread in one gloved hand and a piece of cheese in the other.

"That's him," said Hall.

"What the devil's this?" came in an angry voice from above the collar of the strange figure.

"Well, Mister," said Jaffers, "I've got to arrest you, head or no head."

"Keep off!" said the stranger, jumping back.

He took off his glove and with it struck Jaffers in the face. In another moment Jaffers had seized him by the handless wrist, and caught his invisible throat. He got a hard kick that made him shout with pain, but he kept his hold. A chair stood in the way, and fell with a crash as they came down together.

"Get hold of his feet," said Jaffers between his teeth to the other men.

When he tried to obey this order, Mr Hall received a great kick in the chest that finished him for a time; and Mr Wadgers, seeing that the headless stranger had rolled over and got on top of Jaffers, went backwards towards the door, and so fell against Mr Huxter and another man coming to help the policeman. Four bottles fell and broke on the floor, filling the room with a powerful smell.

"I give in," said the stranger, though he had thrown Jaffers down; and in another moment he stood up, shaking, breathless. A strange thing, he looked, without head or hands. His voice seemed to come out of nothing.

Jaffers also got up.

The stranger ran his arm down his coat, and the buttons to which his empty sleeve pointed became undone. Then he bent down and seemed to touch his shoes.

"Why!" said Huxter suddenly, "That's not a man at all. It's just empty clothes. Look! You can see down his collar and his shirt. I could put my arm——"

He stretched out his hand; it seemed to meet something in the air, and he pulled it back with a sharp cry of surprise.

"I wish you'd keep your fingers out of my eye," shouted the voice in anger. "The fact is, I'm all here — head, hands, legs, and all the rest of it, but it happens I'm invisible. But that's no reason why you should put your fingers in my eye, is it?"

The suit of clothes, now all unbuttoned, stood up.

Several other men had now come into the room, so that it was crowded.

"Invisible, eh?" said Huxter. "Who ever heard of such a——"

"It's strange, perhaps, but it's not a crime. Why am I attacked by a policeman in this way?"

"Ah! That's different," said Jaffers. "I can't see you, but I have orders to arrest you, not because you can't be seen, but because a house has been robbed."

"Well?"

"And it looks as if——"

"Nonsense," said the Invisible Man.

"I hope so, sir. But I've got my orders."

Suddenly the man sat down, and before anyone could think of stopping him, he had thrown off all his clothes except his shirt.

"Here, stop that," said Jaffers suddenly. "Hold him," he cried. "If he gets his shirt off——"

"Hold him," shouted everyone, and there was a rush at the white shirt, which was now all that could be seen of the stranger.

The shirt sleeve struck a blow in Hall's face that sent him backward into old Toothsome, the gravedigger, and in another moment the shirt was lifted up, just like a shirt that is being pulled over a man's head. Jaffers tore at it but only helped to pull it off. He was struck in the mouth out of the air, and lifted his stick and hit Teddy Henfrey hard on the top of his head.

"Look out!" cried everybody, hitting everywhere at nothing. "Hold him! Shut the door! Don't let him go! I've got something! Here he is!" Everybody was being hit at once, falling on one another. Sandy Wadgers opened the door and they fell out. The hitting went on. One man had a tooth broken, another a swollen ear. Jaffers was struck under the jaw. He caught at something hard that stood between him and Huxter. Then the whole mass of struggling, excited men fell out into the crowded hall.

The battle moved quickly to the house door. There were excited cries of "Hold him!", "Invisible!", and a young man, a stranger to the place, rushed in, caught something, missed his hold, and fell over another man's body. Halfway across the road a woman fainted as something pushed past her, a dog ran growling into Huxter's yard, and with that the Invisible Man was gone.

For a moment people stood, not knowing what to do. And then they ran, scattered as the wind scatters dead leaves.

But Jaffers lay quite still, face upward and knees bent.

Chapter 8

On the Road

Mr Thomas Marvel, a tramp, had removed his boots and was sitting by the roadside airing his feet and looking sadly at his toes. They were the best boots he had worn for a long time, but he hated them for their ugliness and their size. "The ugliest boots in the whole world, I should think," he said.

"They're boots, anyway." said a Voice.

"Yes," Mr Marvel agreed. "They were given to me. Too large. I'm tired of them. That's why I've been begging for boots, boots, boots everywhere, but no one has any to give away."

"H'm," said the Voice.

"No. I've been begging for boots round here for ten years. I've got all my boots around here, and now look at them — they're the best they can find for me."

He turned his head over his shoulder to look at the boots of the speaker — but they weren't there. There were neither boots nor legs — nothing.

"Where are you?" he asked. He saw the road, the open country, but no sign of any man except himself. "Am I mad? I must be seeing things."

"No, you aren't," said the Voice. "Don't be frightened."

"Frightened, frightened!" said Mr Marvel. "Come here. Where are you?"

"Don't be frightened," said the Voice.

"You'll be frightened soon. Let me get hold of you. Are you buried?"

There was no answer. Mr Marvel began to put on his coat.

"I could have sworn I heard a voice."

"So you did."

"It's there again," said Mr Marvel, closing his eyes and running his hand across his forehead. "I must have gone mad."

"Don't be a fool," said the Voice. "You think I'm just in your imagination — just in your mind?"

"What else can you be?" said Mr Marvel, rubbing the back of his neck.

"Very well," said the Voice, "I'm going to throw stones at you until you think differently."

"But where are you?"

The Voice made no answer. A stone came whistling through the empty air and just missed Mr Marvel's shoulder. He turned round and saw a stone jump up into the air, hang there for a moment, and fall at his feet. Another came and hit his bare toes, which made Mr Marvel cry aloud. Then he started to run, fell over something unseen, and came to rest sitting by the road.

"*Now*," said the Voice, "am I just in your mind?"

Mr Marvel struggled to his feet, and was immediately rolled over again. He lay quiet for a moment.

"If you struggle any more," said the Voice, "I'll throw this stone at your head."

"I'm finished," said Mr Thomas Marvel, sitting up and taking his wounded toe in his hand. "I don't understand it. Stones throwing themselves. Stones talking. I'm finished."

"It's very simple," said the Voice. "I'm an invisible man."

"Tell me something I *don't* know," said Mr Marvel, white with the pain. "Where you're hidden — how you do it — I don't know. I'm beaten."

"I'm invisible," said the Voice. "That's what I want you to understand."

"Anyone can see that. There's no need for you to be so angry. Now then. Give us an idea. Where are you hidden?"

"I'm invisible. That's the point. And what I want you to understand is this——"

"But where are you?" interrupted Mr Marvel.

"Here — six yards in front of you."

"Oh, no! I'm not blind. You'll be telling me next you're just thin air."

"Yes. I am — thin air. You're looking through me."

"What! Isn't there anything in you?"

"I am just a human being — solid, needing food and drink, needing clothes, too . . . But I'm invisible. You see? Invisible. Simple idea. Invisible."

"What, are you real?"

"Yes, real."

"Let me feel your hand," said Marvel, "if you are real."

He felt with his fingers the hand that had closed round his wrist and his touch went up the arm, found a chest, and touched a bearded face.

Mr Marvel's own face showed shock and surprise.

"Of course, all this isn't half so strange as you think," said the Invisible Man.

"It's quite strange enough for me," said Mr Marvel. "How do you manage it? How is it done?"

"It's a very long story. And besides——"

"I tell you, the whole business is — I can't understand," said Mr Marvel.

"What I want to say now is this: I need help. I need help immediately. I came on you suddenly. I was wandering around helpless, without clothes. And I saw you——"

"Oh, *Lord*!" said Mr Marvel.

"I came up behind you, stopped, went on, then stopped again. 'Here,' I said to myself, 'is the man for me.' So I turned and came back to you. You. And——"

"Oh, *Lord*!" said Mr Marvel. "May I ask: What does it feel like? And what kind of help do you need? Invisible!"

"I want you to help me get clothes and shelter, and then other things.

I've left those things long enough. If you won't — well! . . . But you will — you *must*."

"Look here," said Mr Marvel. "Don't knock me about any more. And let me go. I must get my breath back. And you've very nearly broken my toe. It's all so unreasonable. Empty earth, empty sky. Nothing visible for miles except Nature. And then comes a voice. A voice out of heaven! And stones. And a hand. Lord!"

"Pull yourself together," said the Voice, "for you have to do the work I want you to do."

Mr Marvel's mouth opened wide, and his eyes were round.

"I've chosen you," said the Voice. "You are the only man except some of those fools down there who knows there is such a thing as an Invisible Man. You have to be my helper. Help me — and I will do great things for you. An Invisible Man is a man of great power." He stopped for a moment to sneeze loudly.

"But if you trick me," he said, "if you fail to do as I tell you——"

He paused and took hold of Mr Marvel's shoulder. Mr Marvel gave a cry of terror at the touch.

"I don't want to trick you," he said, moving away from the fingers. "Don't think that, whatever you do. All I want to do is help you — just tell me what I have got to do. Whatever you want done, I shall be pleased to do it."

At about four o'clock, a stranger entered the village from the direction of the hills. He was a short, fat person in a dirty old hat, and he seemed to be very much out of breath. There was fear in his face, and he seemed to be talking to himself. Some of the village men noticed him. Mr Huxter saw him go up the steps of the inn, and turn towards the parlour. Mr Huxter heard voices from the parlour telling the man that he must not go in.

"That room's private!" said Mr Hall, and the stranger shut the door and went into the bar.

A few minutes later he came out again, rubbing his mouth as if he had been having a drink. He stood looking around him for a few moments, and then walked towards the gates of the yard, where the parlour window was. He leant against one of the gateposts and took out a short pipe. Although he seemed calm, his hands were trembling.

Suddenly he put the pipe back in his pocket and disappeared into the yard. Immediately Mr Huxter, guessing that the man was a thief, ran out of his shop to stop him. As he did so, Mr Marvel reappeared, carrying some clothes tied together in one hand and three books in the other. As soon as he saw Huxter he turned and began to run towards the hill road.

"Stop thief!" cried Huxter, and set off after him.

Mr Huxter had hardly gone any distance at all when something seized his leg and sent him flying through the air. He saw the ground suddenly move towards to his face, and then — nothing.

Chapter 9

In the Coach and Horses

At the time when Mr Marvel went into the inn, Mr Cuss and Mr Bunting were in the parlour, searching the stranger's property in the hope of finding something to explain the events of the morning. Jaffers had recovered from his fall and had gone home. Mrs Hall had tidied the stranger's clothes and put them away. And under the window where the stranger did his work, Mr Cuss found three big books.

"Now," said Cuss, "we shall learn something."

But when they opened the books they could read nothing. Cuss turned the pages.

"Dear me," he said, "I can't understand."

"No pictures, nothing to show——?" asked Mr Bunting.

"See for yourself," said Mr Cuss, "it's all Greek or Russian or some other language."

The door opened suddenly. Both men looked round. It was Mr Marvel. He held the door open for a moment.

"I beg your pardon," he said.

"Please shut that door," said Mr Cuss, and Mr Marvel went out.

"My nerves — my nerves are in pieces today," said Mr Cuss. "It made me jump when the door opened like that."

Mr Bunting smiled. "Now let us look at the books again. It's true that strange things have been happening in the village. But of course I can't believe in an invisible man. I *can't*."

"No. Though I tell you I saw right down his sleeve."

"But are you sure?" said Mr Bunting. "Are you quite sure?"

"Quite. I've said so. There's no doubt at all. Now let's look at these books."

They turned over the pages, unable to read a word of their strange language. Suddenly Mr Bunting felt something take hold of the back of his neck. He was unable to lift his head.

"Don't move, little men, or I'll knock your brains out."

Mr Bunting looked at Cuss, whose face had turned white with fear.

"I am sorry to be rough," said the Voice. "Since when did you learn to look through other men's possessions?"

Two noses struck the table. "To come unasked into a stranger's private room! Listen. I am a strong man. I could kill you both and escape unseen, if I wanted to. If I let you go, you must promise to do as I tell you."

"Yes," said Mr Bunting.

Then the hands let their necks go and the two men sat up, now very red in the face.

"Don't move," said the Voice. "Here's the poker, you see."

They saw the poker dance in the air. It touched Mr Bunting's nose.

"Now, where are my clothes? Just now, though the days are quite warm enough for an invisible man to run about without anything on, the evenings are cold. I want some clothes. And I must also have those three books."

Chapter 10

The Invisible Man Loses His Temper

While these things were going on in the parlour, and while Mr Huxter was watching Mr Marvel as he leaned smoking his pipe against the gate, Mr Hall and Teddy Henfrey stood talking nearby.

Suddenly there came a loud knock on the door of the parlour, a cry, and then — silence.

"Hel-lo!" said Teddy Henfrey.

"Hel-lo!" from the bar.

Mr Hall and Teddy looked at the door.

"Something's wrong," said Hall.

For a long time they listened. Strange noises were coming from behind the closed door, as if something was falling about. Then a sharp cry.

"No! No, you don't." Then silence.

"What's that?" exclaimed Henfrey in a low voice.

"Is everything all right there?" called Hall.

"Quite ri-ight," came Mr Bunting's voice, "qui-ite! Don't come in!"

They stood listening.

"I *can't*," they heard Mr Bunting say. "I tell you, sir, I will not."

"Who's that speaking now?" asked Henfrey.

"Mr Cuss, I suppose," said Hall. "Can you hear anything?"

Silence.

"Someone is throwing the table around," said Hall.

Mrs Hall appeared behind the bar. When they told her, she would not believe anything strange was happening. Perhaps they were moving the chairs and table.

"Didn't I hear the window?" said Henfrey.

"What window?" asked Mrs Hall.

"The parlour window," said Henfrey.

Everyone stood listening. Mrs Hall, looking straight in front of her, saw, without seeing, the bright shape of the inn door, the white road, and Huxter's shop-front shining in the June sun. Suddenly Huxter's door opened, and Huxter appeared, his eyes staring with excitement, his arms waving in the air.

"Stop thief!" cried Huxter, and he ran towards the yard gates and disappeared.

At the same time a noise came from the parlour, and there was the sound of windows being closed.

Hall, Henfrey, and everyone in the bar rushed out into the street. They saw someone run round the corner towards the hill road, and Mr Huxter jump into the air and fall on his face and shoulder. Hall and two workmen ran down the street and saw Mr Marvel disappearing past the church wall.

But Hall had hardly run twelve yards when he gave a loud shout and fell on his side, pulling one of the workmen with him. The second workman came up, and he too was knocked down. Then came the rush of the village crowd. The first man was surprised to see Huxter and Hall on the ground. Suddenly something happened to his feet, and he was lying on his back, the crowd was falling over him, and he was being sworn at by a number of angry people.

When Hall, Henfrey and the workmen ran out of the house, Mrs Hall had remained in the bar. Suddenly the parlour door was opened, Mr Cuss appeared and, without looking at her, rushed down the steps towards the corner of the street.

"Hold him!" he cried. "Don't let him drop those books and clothes! You can see him so long as he holds them."

He knew nothing of Marvel; for the Invisible Man had handed over the books and clothes to him in the yard. The face of Mr Cuss was angry and determined, but there was something wrong with his clothes: he was wearing a tablecloth.

"Hold him!" he shouted. "He's got my trousers — and all the vicar's clothes!"

Coming round the corner to join the crowd, he was knocked off his feet and lay kicking on the ground. Somebody stepped on his finger. He struggled to his feet, something knocked against him and threw him on his knees again, and he saw that everyone was running back to the village. He rose again, and was hit behind the ear. He set off straight back to the village inn as fast as he could run, and on his way jumped over the body of Huxter, who was now sitting up.

Behind him, as he was halfway up the inn steps, he heard a sudden cry of anger above the noise, and the sound of someone being struck in the face. He knew the voice as that of the Invisible Man.

In another moment Mr Cuss was back in the parlour.

"He's coming back, Bunting!" he said, rushing in. "Save yourself!"

Mr Bunting was standing in the window, trying to dress himself in the curtains and a newspaper.

"Who's coming?" he said, so surprised that his dress nearly fell off him.

"The Invisible Man!" said Cuss, and rushed to the window. "We'd better move — quick. He's fighting like a madman!"

In another moment he was out in the yard.

Mr Bunting heard a frightful struggle in the passage of the inn, and decided to leave. He climbed out of the window, and ran up the village street as fast as his fat little legs could carry him.

Chapter 11

Mr Marvel Tries to Say No

Mr Marvel was walking painfully through the thick woods on the road to Bramblehurst. He looked very unhappy and was carrying three books and some clothes wrapped in a blue tablecloth. A Voice went with him and he was held tightly by unseen hands.

"If you try to escape again," said the Voice, "I will kill you."

"I didn't try to escape," said Mr Marvel.

The Voice swore a few times and then stopped. Mr Marvel, who was not used to so much work, was very tired. There was silence for a time. Then, "I shall have to make use of you. You are a poor creature, but I must."

"Yes, I am," said Marvel.

"You are," said the Voice.

"I'm not strong," said Marvel. Then after a short silence he repeated, "I'm not strong. I've got a weak heart. I can't do what you want."

"I'll make you," said the Voice.

"I wish I was dead," said Marvel.

"Go on! Walk! Move!" said the Voice.

"It's cruel," said Marvel.

"Be quiet," said the Voice. "I'll see that you're all right. But be quiet. I want to think."

Soon they saw the lights of a village.

"I shall keep my hand on your shoulder," said the Voice. "Go straight through the village, and don't try to say anything to anybody."

Chapter 12

At Port Stowe

At ten o'clock the next morning Mr Marvel, dirty, tired, and worried, sat outside a little inn at Port Stowe. Beside him were the books, but now they were tied up with string. He had left the clothes in the woods beyond Bramblehurst. Mr Marvel sat on a wooden seat and, although no one took any notice of him, he seemed excited.

When he had been sitting for nearly an hour an old sailor, with a newspaper in his hand, came out of the inn and sat down beside him.

"Pleasant day," said the sailor.

Mr Marvel looked around him with eyes that were full of terror. "Very," he replied.

The sailor looked around him as if he had nothing to do, and then at Mr Marvel's dusty clothes and the books beside him. He had heard the sound of money being dropped into a pocket, and thought that Mr Marvel did not look like a man who would carry much money.

"Books?" he said suddenly.

Mr Marvel jumped and looked at them. "Oh, yes," he said. "Yes, they're books."

"There are some strange things in books," said the sailor.

"There are," said Mr Marvel.

"And some strange things out of them," said the sailor.

"True," said Mr Marvel.

"There are some strange things in newspapers, for example," said the sailor.

"There are."

"In *this* newspaper," said the sailor.

"Ah!" said Mr Marvel.

"There's a story," said the sailor, "there's a story about an Invisible Man." And he told Mr Marvel as much of the story as the newspaper contained. "I don't like it," he said. "He might be anywhere, might be here at this moment listening to us. And just think, if he wanted to steal or kill, what is there to stop him?"

Mr Marvel seemed to be listening for the least sound.

"Ah — and — well——" he said. And lowering his voice, "I know something about this Invisible Man."

"Oh," said the sailor, "you?"

"Yes," said Mr Marvel, "me."

The sailor did not seem to believe Mr Marvel.

"It happened like this," Mr Marvel began, and then his expression changed suddenly.

"Ow!" he said. He rose stiffly from his seat, as if in pain.

"What's the matter?" said the sailor.

"I — I think I must be going," said Mr Marvel.

"But you were just going to tell me about this Invisible Man," said the sailor.

Mr Marvel seemed to think carefully.

"A lie," said a Voice.

"It's a lie," said Mr Marvel.

"But it's in the paper," said the sailor.

"Yes," said Mr Marvel loudly, "but it's a lie. I know the man who started it. There isn't any Invisible Man at all."

"But this paper? D'you mean to say——?"

"Not a word of truth in it," said Mr Marvel firmly.

The sailor stared, the paper in his hand. Mr Marvel turned round.

"Wait a bit," said the sailor, rising and speaking slowly. "D'you mean to say——?"

"I do," said Mr Marvel.

"Then why did you let me go on and tell you all this, then? What do you mean by letting a man make a fool of himself like that for, eh?"

"Come along," said a Voice, and Mr Marvel was suddenly turned round and he started marching off in a strange, jumpy manner.

"Silly devil," said the sailor, legs wide apart, watching the little man go. "I'll show you, you silly fool! It's here in the paper!"

And there was another strange thing he was soon to hear about, that had happened quite close to him. And that was a "hand full of money" travelling by itself along by the wall. A sailor friend had seen this strange sight that very morning. He had tried to take the money and had been knocked down by an unseen hand, and when he had got to his feet the money had disappeared.

The story of the flying money was true. And all round that neighbourhood, even from the bank, from shops and inns, money had quietly walked away. And it had found its way into Mr Marvel's pocket, so the sailor had heard.

Chapter 13

The Man in a Hurry

In the early evening time, Dr Kemp was sitting in his study on the hill above Burdock. It was a pleasant little upstairs room, with three windows — north, west, and south — with bookshelves crowded with books and with a broad writing table. Dr Kemp was a tall, thin man of about thirty-five, with fair hair. He was writing.

His eye, soon wandering from his work, caught the sunset behind the hill opposite his house. For a minute, perhaps, he sat, pen in mouth, admiring the rich golden colour, and then he saw the little figure of a man running over the hill towards him. He was a shortish little man, in a dirty old hat, and he was running fast.

Dr Kemp got up, went to the window, and stared at the hillside and the dark little figure running down it. "He seems to be in a hurry," said Dr Kemp to himself.

Then the running man was hidden behind some houses; he came into sight and disappeared again — still running.

But those who were nearer to him saw the terror in his face. He looked neither to the right nor left, but his wide eyes stared straight down the hill to where the lamps were being lit and there were people crowding together in the street. Everybody he passed stopped and began staring up and down the road, and asking one another, half afraid, why the man was running so hard.

And then, far up the hill, a dog playing in the road growled and ran under a gate, and something — a wind — a noise of feet, a sound like heavy breathing — rushed by.

People cried out. People jumped off the footpath. They shouted as the thing rushed past them down the hill, and they were still shouting in the street before Marvel was halfway there. They were running into houses with the news and shutting the doors behind them. He heard it, and ran even faster. Fear came hurrying by, rushed ahead of him, and in a moment had seized the town.

"*The Invisible Man* is coming! *The Invisible Man!*"

Chapter 14

In the Happy Cricketers

At the bottom of the hill was an inn called the Happy Cricketers. Inside, the barman leant his fat red arms on the table and talked about horses with a cabman, while a black-bearded man who spoke like an American ate bread and cheese and talked to a policeman.

"What's the shouting about?" said the cabman, trying to see up the hill over the dirty yellow curtains in the low window of the inn. Somebody ran past outside.

"Fire, perhaps," said the barman.

The door was pushed open, and Marvel, crying, his hat gone, the neck of his coat torn open, rushed in and tried to shut the door. It was held half open by a door-stop.

"Coming!" he cried, his voice cracked with terror. "He's coming. The Invisible Man! After me. Help! Help! Help!"

"Shut the doors," said the policeman. "Who's coming? What's the matter?" He went to the door and removed the door-stop, and the door shut with a bang. The man with the beard closed the other door.

"Let me hide," said Marvel, with tears running down his face. "Let me hide. Lock me in somewhere. I tell you he's after me. I escaped. He said he'd kill me, and he will."

"You're safe," said the man with the black beard. "The door's shut. What's it all about?"

"Let me hide," said Marvel, and cried aloud as a blow suddenly made the locked door shake. The blow was followed by a hurried knocking and a shouting outside.

"Hello," cried the policeman, "who's there?"

"He'll kill me," shouted Mr Marvel, "he's got a knife or something. Don't open the door. *Please* don't open the door. *Where* shall I hide?"

"Is this the Invisible Man, then?" asked the black-bearded man, with one hand behind him. "I think it's about time we saw him."

The window of the inn was suddenly broken in, and there were shouts, and people running about in the street. The policeman had been standing on a chair, looking out of the window to see who was at the door. He got down. "That's who it is," he said. The barman stood in front of the parlour door, where Mr Marvel was now locked in, and stared at the broken window. Then he came round to the two other men.

Everything was suddenly quiet. "I wish I had my stick," said the policeman. "If we open the door, he'll come in. Nothing can stop him."

"Don't be in too much of a hurry about that door," said the cabman anxiously.

"Unlock it," said the man with the black beard, "and if he comes . . ." He showed them the revolver in his hand.

"That won't do," said the policeman; "that's murder."

"I know what country I'm in," said the man with the beard. "I'm going to shoot at his legs. Unlock it."

"Not with that thing going off behind me," said the barman.

"Very well," said the man with the black beard. He stepped forward with his gun ready, and unlocked the door himself. Barman, cabman and policeman turned around.

"Come in," said the bearded man in a low voice, standing back and facing the door with his gun behind him. No one came in, and the door remained closed.

"Are all the doors of the house shut?" asked Marvel, five minutes later. "He's going round to the back."

"There's the yard door," said the barman, "and the private door. The yard door——"

He rushed out of the bar.

In a minute he appeared again with a long sharp knife in his hand. "The yard door was open," he said.

"He may be in the house now," said the cabman.

The man with the beard put the gun back in his pocket. As he did so, the door opened, something rushed past them, and the parlour door burst open. They heard Marvel cry out and ran to his rescue. The bearded man's revolver went off, and the mirror at the back of the parlour came crashing down on the floor.

As the barman came into the room, he saw Marvel struggling against the door that led to the yard and kitchen. The door flew open and Marvel was dragged into the kitchen.

The policeman, who had been trying to pass the barman, rushed in, followed by the cabman, caught hold of the invisible hand that held Marvel, was hit in the face and fell down. Then the cabman took hold of something.

"I've got him," said the cabman.

"Here he is!" said the barman.

Mr Marvel suddenly dropped to the ground, and made an attempt to hide behind the legs of the fighting men. The struggle went backwards and forwards near the door. The voice of the Invisible Man was heard for the first time, as the policeman stepped on his foot. Then he cried out, and his arms flew out. The cabman was suddenly knocked to the ground by a kick in the stomach. The door into the bar parlour from the kitchen shut with a bang as Mr Marvel escaped through it. The men in the kitchen found themselves struggling with empty air.

"Where's he gone?" cried the man with the beard. "Out?"

"This way," said the policeman, stepping into the yard and stopping.

A large stone flew by his head and fell on the kitchen table.

"I'll show him," shouted the man with the black beard and he fired five rapid shots in the direction the stone had come from. As he fired, the man with the beard moved his hand slightly, so that his shots went from one side to the other of the narrow yard.

A silence followed. "Come along," he said, "and feel around for his body."

Chapter 15

Dr Kemp's Visitor

Dr Kemp was writing in his study when he heard the shots.

Crack, crack, crack, they came, one after the other.

"Hello!" said Dr Kemp to himself, putting his pen into his mouth again and listening. "Who's letting off guns in Burdock? What are they doing now?"

He went to the south window, threw it up and, leaning out, stared down on the town. "It looks like a crowd down by the Happy Cricketers," he said to himself. Then his eyes wandered over the town to far away where the ships' lights shone. The moon in its first quarter hung over the hill to the west, and the stars were clear and bright.

Five minutes later, Dr Kemp pulled down the window again, and returned to his writing desk.

It must have been about an hour after this that the front-door bell rang. He sat listening. He heard the servant go to the door, and waited for the sound of her feet on the staircase, but she did not come.

"What was that about?" Dr Kemp asked himself.

He tried to go on with his work, failed, and went downstairs. He rang the bell and called to the servant as she appeared in the hall.

"Was that a letter?" he asked.

"Only the bell ringing, sir, and no one there," she answered.

"I'm restless tonight," he said to himself. He went back to his study.

Soon afterwards he was hard at work again, and his room was silent except for the sounds of the clock and his pen moving over the paper.

It was two o'clock before he had finished his work for the night. He rose and went upstairs to bed. When he had taken off his coat and shirt, he felt thirsty. He took a lamp and went down to the dining room in search of a drink.

Dr Kemp's scientific work had trained him to notice things quickly. As he crossed the hall, he saw a dark spot on the floor near the stairs. He went on upstairs, and then he asked himself what the dark spot on the floor might be. He went back to the hall, and, bending down, touched the spot. It looked and felt like drying blood.

He returned upstairs, looking around him and thinking about the blood spot. Then suddenly he saw something which made him stop. There was blood on the handle of his door.

He looked at his own hand. It was quite clean. Then he remembered that the door of his room had been open when he came down from his study, and that he had not touched the handle at all. He went straight into his bedroom, his face quite calm — perhaps a little more determined than usual . . . He looked at the bed. There was a pool of blood, and the sheet was torn. He had not noticed this when he had been in the room before. The other side of the bed looked as if someone had been lying on it.

Then he seemed to hear a low voice say, "Help me! — Kemp!" But Dr Kemp did not believe in "voices".

He stood staring at the sheets. Was it really a voice? He looked around him again, and noticed nothing. But he clearly heard something move across the room. A strange feeling came over him. He closed the door of the room and came forward. Suddenly, with a shock, he saw a bloody bandage hanging in the air between him and the bed.

He stared at it in surprise. It was an empty bandage — a bandage properly tied, but quite empty. He would have moved forward to take hold of it, but a touch stopped him and a voice spoke quite close to him.

"Kemp!" said the Voice.

"Eh!" said Kemp, with his mouth open.

Said the Voice, "I'm an invisible man."

Kemp made no answer for a moment or two, but simply stared at the bandage. "The Invisible Man?" he said at last.

"I'm an invisible man," repeated the Voice.

"I thought it was a lie," he said. "Have you got a bandage on?" he asked.

"Yes," said the Invisible Man.

"Oh!" said Kemp, and then, "I say! But this is nonsense. It's some trick." He stepped forward suddenly, stretched out his hand towards the bandage and met invisible fingers.

"Keep steady, Kemp, in God's name! I want help badly. Stop!"

The hand seized his arm. He struck at it. "Kemp!" cried the Voice. "Kemp, keep still!"

A desire to free himself took hold of Kemp. But the hand held his shoulder, and he was suddenly pushed and fell backwards upon the bed. He opened his mouth to shout, and the corner of the sheet was pushed between his teeth. The Invisible Man held him down, but his arms were free, and he hit back fiercely.

"Listen to reason, will you?" said the Invisible Man. "By heaven, you'll make me mad! Stop struggling and lie still! Lie still!"

Kemp struggled for another moment, and then lay still.

"Let me get up," he said. "I'll stay where I am. And let me sit quiet for a minute."

He sat up and felt his neck.

"I'm just an ordinary man — a man you used to know — made invisible. Do you remember Griffin?"

"Griffin?" repeated Kemp.

"Griffin," answered the Voice. "A younger student than you."

"What has this to do with Griffin?"

"I am Griffin."

Kemp laughed. "It's too much of a shock," he said. "But what devil's work can make a man invisible?"

"It's no devil's work. It's honest and simple enough."

"It's terrible!" said Kemp. "How on earth——?"

"I'm wounded and in pain, and tired . . . Great God! Kemp, you are a man. Keep calm. Give me some food and drink, and let me sit down here."

Kemp stared at the bandage as it moved across the room, then saw a chair slide along the floor and come to rest near the bed. It made a noise, and the seat sank slightly. He rubbed his eyes and felt his neck again.

"This beats magic," he said, and laughed stupidly.

"That's better. Thank heaven, you're becoming sensible!"

"Or silly," said Kemp, and rubbed his eyes again.

"Give me something to drink. I'm nearly dead."

"It didn't feel like that. Where are you? If I get up, shall I run into you? *There*! All right. A drink . . . Here. Where shall I give it you?"

Kemp felt the glass taken out of his hand. He let it go into the air. It came to rest just in front of the chair seat. He stared at it.

"This . . . I don't believe it . . . I must be mad."

"Nonsense!" said the Voice. "Listen to me. I'm hungry, and the night is cold to a man with no clothes on."

"Food?" offered Kemp.

The glass emptied itself.

"Yes," said the Invisible Man, putting it down. "Can you give me something to wear?"

Kemp found some clothes. "These?" he asked.

They were taken from him. They hung in the air, buttoned themselves and sat down in the chair.

"The maddest thing I've ever seen in my life," said Kemp.

"Some food?"

Kemp went to the kitchen for some bread and some meat, returned and put them on a table in front of his guest.

"Never mind about a knife," said the Invisible Man: and a piece of meat hung in the air and disappeared with a sound of eating.

"I always like to have clothes on when I eat," said the Voice.

"Is your arm all right?"

"Not very painful."

"It's all mad, as mad as can be."

"Quite reasonable," said the Invisible Man.

"But how's it done?" began Kemp. "What were the shots?" he asked. "How did the shooting begin?"

"There was a man — I tried to make him help me! — who tried to steal my money. And he has stolen it."

"Is he invisible too?"

"No."

"Well?"

"Can't I have some more to eat before I tell you all about it? I'm hungry — in pain. And you want me to tell stories!"

Kemp got up. "*You* didn't do any shooting?" he asked.

"Not me," said his visitor. "Some fool fired, a man I'd never seen before. A lot of them got frightened. They all got frightened of me. I say — I want more to eat than this, Kemp."

"I'll see whether there's anything more to eat downstairs," said Kemp. "Not much, I'm afraid."

Kemp found some more food. And when his guest had eaten, he told him to try to get some sleep.

Though the Invisible Man was wounded and tired, he refused to accept Kemp's word that no one would try to seize him. He examined the two windows of the bedroom, pulled up the blinds and opened the windows to see whether it was possible to get out that way, as Kemp had told him. Outside the night was very quiet and still, and the new moon was setting over the hill. Then he examined the key of the bedroom door. At last he said he was satisfied. He stood by the fireside and Kemp heard his breathing relax.

"I'm sorry," said the Invisible Man, "if I cannot tell you all that I've done tonight, but I'm so tired. It's foolish, no doubt. It's horrible! But, believe me, Kemp, in spite of your arguments, it's quite a possible thing. I've made a discovery. I intended to keep it secret. I can't. I must have someone to help me. And you . . . We can do such great things together . . . But tomorrow. Now, Kemp, I feel as though I must sleep or die."

They said goodnight to each other, and Kemp stayed in his room, thinking. He picked up a newspaper and found that it was full of reports of the Invisible Man. As he read, he began to feel afraid of what his guest might do if he was allowed to stay free. He wrote a note and addressed it to "Colonel Adye, Port Burdock".

Chapter 16

How to Become Invisible

The next morning Kemp heard a loud noise and went to see his guest.

"What's the matter?" asked Kemp, when the Invisible Man let him in.

"Nothing," was the answer.

"But, good heavens! What was that crash?"

"I lost my temper," said the Invisible Man. "I forgot this arm; and it's sore."

"You're rather in the habit of losing your temper."

"I am."

"Your story is in the papers," Kemp said.

The Invisible Man swore.

"Come and have some breakfast," said Kemp, leading the way. "Before we can do anything else," he went on, "I must understand a little more about you." He had sat down, with the air of a man who means to talk seriously.

"It's simple enough," said Griffin.

"No doubt it's simple enough to you, but——" Kemp laughed.

"Well, yes, to me it seemed strange at first, no doubt. But we can still do great things! I found the secret first at Chesilstowe College."

"Chesilstowe?"

"I went there after I left London. You know I have always been interested in light."

"Ah!"

"I said: 'I will give my life to this. This is worth my trouble.' You know what fools we are at twenty-two."

"Fools then and fools now," said Kemp.

"As though just knowing could satisfy a man! I saw a way to change the human body, or any other kind of body . . ." And then the strange man, or rather the clothes of a man, sitting opposite Kemp, explained how a student of science had disappeared.

"If you take a small piece of glass and crush it into powder, the powder is white and solid like salt. You can't see through it. Human flesh, white paper, cloth, hair, are really made of a kind of powder. The tiny grains of powder break up the light which shines on them, so that it can't shine *through* them, and that is why we can see flesh and paper. Now, if you could smooth the broken grains of powder so that they would not break up the light, they would no longer look solid. The light would shine through them, just as now the sun is shining through me. You can try it with a piece of white paper and a drop of oil. Pour a little oil on the paper and things will begin to show through it. If the oil is good enough and the paper is bad enough, you will be able to see through the paper to the print on the other side. That is because the oil is smooth and it smoothes out the rough surfaces of each little grain of the powder.

"Well, I found something which would do to human flesh what the oil does to the paper, and would do it so perfectly that there is no tiny part of my body which holds up the light. It is as if you had taken powdered glass and turned it back into the unbroken glass of that window."

The explanation, as always between two scientists, led to all kinds of questions. Kemp was so surprised at the story that he nearly forgot that his friend was invisible.

"Yes," said the Voice, "I had found it all. The way was open — and then — then after years of care and working in secret — then I knew that I could do nothing. I knew, and I was helpless. And that was after three years of secrecy and hard work."

"Why could you do nothing?" asked Kemp.

"I had no money," said the Invisible Man, and went to stare out of the window.

He turned round. "I robbed the old man — robbed my father. The money was not his, and he shot himself."

Chapter 17

The Experiment

For a moment Kemp sat in silence, staring at the back of the headless figure at the window. Then he rose, took the Invisible Man's arm and turned him away from the view.

"You're tired," he said, "and while I'm sitting down, you walk around. Have my chair."

He got up and stood between Griffin and the nearest window.

For a time Griffin sat silently, and then he went on with his story.

"I'd already left the College," he said, "when that happened. It was last December. I had taken a room in London, in a big house in Great Portland Street.

"It was all like a dream, that short visit to my father in my old home. When I returned to my room it seemed like waking from a dream to reality. Here were the things I knew and loved. Here was the equipment; the experiments were arranged and waiting. And now there was hardly any difficulty left, beyond the planning of details.

"I will tell you, Kemp, sooner or later, all the complicated details. We need not talk about that now. For the most part, except for certain words I chose to remember, they are written in those books that that tramp has hidden, in a way that only I can understand. We must hunt him down.

"First I tried some white wool. It was the strangest thing in the world to see it lose its substance, like smoke, and disappear. I could hardly believe I had done it. I put my hand into the emptiness and there was the thing as solid as ever. I felt it, and threw it on the floor. I had a little trouble finding it again.

"And then I heard a noise behind me and, turning, saw a white cat, very dirty, outside the window. A thought came into my head. 'Everything is ready for you,' I said, and went to the window, opened it, and called softly. She came in. The poor creature was thirsty and I gave her some milk. After that she went smelling round the room, plainly with the idea of making herself at home. The invisible wool upset her a bit; you should have seen her attack it! But I made her comfortable on my bed."

"And then you made the cat invisible?"

"Yes: it took four hours."

"You don't mean to say there's an Invisible Cat in the world?" said Kemp.

"If it hasn't been killed," said the Invisible Man. "Why not?"

"Why not?" repeated Kemp. "Go on."

He was silent for a few minutes and then continued. "My only clear thought," he said, "was that the thing had to be completed. And it had to be done soon, for I had little money left. After a time I ate some food and went to sleep in my clothes on my bed.

"I was woken by a loud knock at the door. It was the owner of my room. He said I had been hurting a cat in the night, he was sure. He wanted to know all about it. I told him there had been no cat in my room. Then the noise of my experiments could be heard all over the house, he said. That was true, certainly. He came into the room, asked me what I was doing, and said it had always been a respectable house. In the end I got angry, pushed him out and shut the door. He made some noise outside, but I didn't listen. After a time he went away.

"But I didn't know what he planned to do, nor even what he had the power to do. To move to new rooms would have meant delay — I had twenty pounds left in the world, most of it in a bank. If he brought the police, my room might be searched. What could I do? Disappear! Of course. It was all done that evening and night.

"There was some pain at first. I felt sick. At times I cried out. I talked aloud to myself. But I did not give up. I shall never forget seeing my hands. They became white as white paper and then, slowly, became like glass. And then — they had disappeared. At first I was weak as a little child, walking on legs I could not see.

"I slept during the morning, pulling a sheet over my eyes to shut out the light, and I was woken again by a knocking. My strength had returned. I sat up and listened and heard talking. Soon the knocking was repeated and voices called. To gain time I answered them. My window opened on to a roof. I stepped through it, closed it, stood outside and watched. The old man and his two sons came into the room.

"You may imagine their surprise at finding the room empty. One of the younger men rushed to the window at once, threw it open and stared out. His eyes and his thick-lipped, bearded face came close to my own. He looked right through me. So did the others. The old man went and looked under the bed.

"While they were all talking together, I came back into the room, slipped past them, and went down the stairs. In one room I found a box of matches, and when they had come down I returned to my own room and set fire to the papers, the bedcovers and the furniture."

"You set the house on fire?"

"Set the house on fire! Yes. It was the only way to hide my tracks."

For the next hour he went on with his story, and Kemp listened. It was the story of how the Invisible Man had got some clothes, how he lived by getting food and drink wherever he could, of the shelter he found and the beds he slept in, until he came to Iping.

Chapter 18

The Plan That Failed

"But now," said Kemp, looking out of the window, "what are we to do?"

He moved nearer to his guest so that he did not see the three men who were coming up the hill road — too slowly, as it seemed to Kemp.

"What were you planning to do, when you were going to Port Burdock? Did you have a plan?"

"I was going to leave the country. But I have rather changed that plan since seeing you. I thought it would be wise, now the weather is hot, to make for the south. Especially as my secret was known, and everyone would be watching for a man all wrapped up like me. You have regular boats from here to France. My idea was to get on board one. Then I could go by train into Spain, or else to Algiers. It wouldn't be difficult. There a man could be invisible all the time, but still live and do things. I was using that tramp as a moneybox and carrier until I decided how to get my books and things sent over to join me."

"That's clear."

"And then he tried to rob me! He *has* hidden my books, Kemp. Hidden my books! If I can get hold of him, I'll——"

"You'd better get the books from him first."

"But where is he? Do you know?"

"He's in the town police station, locked up, at his own request, in the strongest room in the place."

"The rat!" said the Invisible Man.

"But that delays your plans a little."

"We must get those books; those books are necessary."

"Certainly," said Kemp, a little anxiously, unsure if he heard footsteps outside. "Certainly we must get those books. But that won't be difficult, if he doesn't know they're for you."

"No," said the Invisible Man, thoughtfully.

Kemp tried to think of something to keep the conversation going, but the Invisible Man continued himself.

"Coming into your house, Kemp," he said, "changes all my plans. For you are a man who can understand. You are a scientist. You have told no one I am here?"

"Not a soul."

"If we are to make any use of being invisible, we must start by killing."

"Killing?" repeated Kemp. "I'm listening to your plan; but I'm not agreeing. Why *killing*?"

"The point is this: they know as well as we do that there is an Invisible Man — and that Invisible Man, Kemp, must now start to rule by terror. Yes; I mean it. To rule by terror. He must take a town like your Burdock and put the fear of God into it. He must give orders. He can do that in many ways. And he must kill everybody who disobeys his orders, and everybody who works against him."

"Really!" said Kemp, no longer listening to Griffin, but to the sound of his front door opening and closing.

The Invisible Man had also heard the sound. "Listen!" he said. "What is that downstairs?"

"Nothing," said Kemp; and suddenly he began to speak loud and fast. "I don't agree to this, Griffin," he said. "Understand me, I don't agree to this. Why do you wish to be alone? Why not tell everyone? Think how much better it would be. You might have a million helpers."

The Invisible Man raised his hand. "There are footsteps coming upstairs," he said.

"Nonsense," said Kemp.

"Let me see," said the Invisible Man, and went to the door and listened.

And then things happened very quickly. Suddenly the clothes sat down and opened as the unseen man began to undress.

Kemp opened the door.

As he opened it, there came sounds of hurrying feet and voices downstairs.

With a quick movement Kemp pushed the Invisible Man back, jumped aside, and shut the door behind him. The key was outside and ready. In another moment Griffin would have been locked in the room, except for one little thing: the key fell noisily on the floor.

Kemp's face became white. He tried to hold the door handle with both hands. For a moment he pulled at it. Then the door opened slightly, but he got it closed again. The second time it was opened a foot, and the clothes came into the opening. Kemp's throat was seized by invisible fingers, and he let go of the handle in order to defend himself. He was forced back and thrown heavily to the floor.

Halfway up the stairs was Colonel Adye, the chief of the Burdock police. He was staring at the sudden appearance of Kemp, followed by the clothes, which danced in the air. He saw Kemp fall and then struggle to his feet. He saw Kemp rush forward, and go down again.

Then suddenly he was struck. By nothing! A great weight, it seemed, jumped on him, and he was thrown down the staircase. An invisible foot stepped on his back, faint steps passed downstairs. He heard the two police officers in the hall shout and run, and the sound of the front door of the house as it shut.

He rolled over and sat up staring. He saw Kemp coming down the staircase, his face white and bleeding.

"My God!" cried Kemp, "I couldn't stop him! He's gone!"

Chapter 19

The Hunt for the Invisible Man

Kemp took some time to explain to Colonel Adye what had happened.

"He's mad," said Kemp. "And evil. He thinks of nothing but his own advantage, his own safety. I've listened this morning to a terrible story of cruelty and pride. He has wounded men. He'll kill them unless we can prevent him. He plans to rule by terror. Nothing can stop him. He's loose outside there now — and he's mad!"

"He must be caught," said Adye. "That's certain."

"But how?" cried Kemp, and suddenly became full of ideas. "You must begin immediately; you must set every man to work; you must prevent him leaving this place. If he gets away, he may go through the country, killing as he goes. The only thing that may keep him here is the thought of finding some books which he values very much. I will tell you about them. There is a man in your police station — Marvel."

"I know," said Adye, "I know. Those books — yes. But the Invisible Man——"

"Says he hasn't got them. But he thinks Marvel has. Now listen! You must prevent him from eating or sleeping — day and night the country must be on the watch for him. Food must be locked up, all food, so that he will have to break into a house or shop to get it. The houses everywhere must be shut against him; for twenty miles round Port Burdock, the whole country must begin hunting and keep on hunting. I tell you, Adye, he's dangerous. Unless he is caught, it's terrible to think of the things that may happen."

"Come along," said Colonel Adye. "Tell me as we go. What else is there we can do?"

In another moment Adye was leading the way downstairs. They

found the front door open and the policemen standing outside staring at empty air.

"He's got away, sir," said one.

"We must tell the police station at once," said Adye. "One of you must go down and report and then come up and meet us — quickly. And now, Kemp, what else?"

"Dogs," said Kemp. "Get dogs. They don't see him, but they smell him. Get dogs."

"Good," said Adye. "We have no suitable dogs, but the prison officers over at Halstead know a man with bloodhounds. What else?"

"Remember," said Kemp, "his food shows. You can see it for some time after he has eaten it, so he has to hide. You must keep on searching in every quiet corner. And put away all weapons — and everything that might be a weapon. He can't carry such things for long. You must hide anything he can pick up and strike men with."

"Good again," said Adye. "We'll find him yet!"

"And the roads——" said Kemp, and hesitated.

"Yes?" said Adye.

"Broken glass," said Kemp. "It's cruel, I know. But think of what he may do!"

Adye drew the air in between his teeth sharply.

"It's cruel. I don't perhaps think we should. But I'll have some broken glass ready. If he is killed, it will be only what he deserves."

"The man is mad, I tell you," said Kemp. "He will do anything. We must catch him by any possible means. He has cut himself off from the human race."

Chapter 20

The Wicksteed Murder

The Invisible Man seems to have rushed out of Kemp's house in blind anger. A little child playing near Kemp's gateway was violently picked up and thrown to one side — so that his leg was broken — and then for some hours the Invisible Man disappeared completely. No one knows where he went or what he did. But we can think of him hurrying through the hot June morning, up the hill and onto the open land behind Port Burdock, and hiding at last in the woods.

There he hid for two hours, while a growing crowd of men was hunting him across the country with dogs, and searching for him in every direction. In the morning he had still been just a story, a terror; in the afternoon, mainly because of Kemp's story, he was shown to be a real enemy who had to be caught and held by force, and the countryside began organising itself very quickly. Before two o'clock, he might still have escaped from the area by boarding a train, but after two that became impossible: every passenger train between Southampton, Winchester, Brighton and Horsham travelled with locked doors, and the goods trains were almost entirely stopped. And in a great circle of twenty miles round Port Burdock, men armed with guns and sticks were soon setting out in groups of three and four, with dogs, to search the roads and fields.

Police on horseback followed the country roads, stopping at every house and warning people to lock their doors and not to go out unless they were armed. All the schools had closed before three o'clock, and the frightened children, keeping together in groups, hurried home. A notice written by Kemp was put up everywhere, telling people clearly what must be done — that the Invisible Man must have neither food nor sleep, that a continuous watch must be kept for signs of him. Before night the whole country was on guard and also before night came news of the murder of Mr Wicksteed.

Somewhere on the road the Invisible Man must have picked up an iron bar. Mr Wicksteed, a quiet, harmless man on his way home from work, had, no doubt, seen an iron bar walking by itself, and had turned to follow it. Perhaps the Invisible Man imagined he was one of the hunters. We only know that he stopped quiet little Mr Wicksteed, attacked him, broke his arm, knocked him down and beat his head to pieces.

Then there is the story of a voice heard by some men in a field, laughing and crying. Across the field it went and was lost. The Invisible Man must have seen the use Kemp had made of his story. He must have found all the houses shut and locked, and seen the groups of men with dogs watching. He knew that he was a hunted man. In the night he must have eaten and slept, for on the last morning he was himself again and ready for his struggle against the world.

Chapter 21

The Attack on Kemp's House

Kemp was reading a strange letter, written in pencil on a dirty sheet of paper.

You have been very clever, though what you gain by it I cannot think. You are against me. For a whole day you have hunted me — you have tried to rob me of a night's rest. But I have had food, I have slept, and we are only beginning. We are only beginning. There is nothing to be done but to start the Terror. This is the first day of the Terror. Port Burdock is no longer under the Queen. Tell your police, and the rest of them; it is under me — the Terror! I am Invisible Man the First. We shall begin with the death of a man named Kemp. He will die today. He may hide himself away, and collect guards around him; Death, the unseen Death, is coming. The game begins. Death starts. If you help him, my people, Death may fall on you too. Today Kemp is to die.

Kemp read this letter twice. "That's his voice!" he said, "and he means it."

He got up slowly, leaving his lunch unfinished — the letter had come by the one o'clock post — and went into his study. He rang the bell for his servant, and told her to go round the house immediately, and see that all the windows were shut. He closed the study windows himself. From a locked drawer in his bedroom he took a little revolver, examined it carefully, and put it into his pocket. He wrote a number of short notes, one to Colonel Adye, and gave them to his servant to take.

"There is no danger to you," he said. He thought for a time and then returned to his meal.

Finally he struck the table. "We will have him!" he said. "He'll go too far."

He went up to his room, carefully shutting every door after him. "It's a game," he said, "a strange game — but I shall win, Mr Griffin," he said.

He stood at the window staring at the hot hillside. "He must get food every day. Did he really sleep last night? Out in the open somewhere? I wish we could get some good cold, wet weather instead of the heat. He may be watching me now."

He went close to the window. Something hit the wall above the window.

"I'm getting worried," said Kemp. But it was five minutes before he went to the window again. "It must have been a bird," he said.

Soon he heard the front-door bell ringing and hurried downstairs. He unchained and unlocked the door, and opened it without showing himself. It was Adye.

"Your servant's been attacked, Kemp," he said round the door.

"What!" exclaimed Kemp.

"She had that note of yours taken away from her. He's very near. Let me in."

Kemp opened the door a few inches, and Adye came in. He stood in the hall, looking at Kemp locking the door.

Kemp swore. "What a fool I was!" he said. "I might have known. Already!"

"What's the matter?" said Adye.

"Look here!" said Kemp, and led the way towards his study. He handed Adye the Invisible Man's letter.

Adye read it, "And you——?" said Adye.

The sound of a breaking window came from upstairs. Adye saw the little revolver half out of Kemp's pocket. "It's a window upstairs!" said Kemp, and led the way up. There came a second noise while they were still on the staircase. When they reached the study they found two of the three windows broken, the floor covered with broken glass, and one big stone lying on the writing table. The two men stopped in the doorway. Kemp swore again, and as he did so the third window broke with a crack like a gunshot, and the broken glass fell into the room.

"What's this for?" said Adye.

"It's beginning," said Kemp.

"There's no way of climbing up here?"

"Not even for a cat," said Kemp.

Stones came flying in and then it sounded as if someone was banging on the windows downstairs. The two men stood outside the study, not knowing what to do.

"I know!" said Adye. "Let me have a stick or something, and I'll go down to the station and get the man with the bloodhounds. They'll find him."

Another window broke.

"You haven't got a revolver?" asked Adye.

Kemp's hand went to his pocket. Then he paused. "I haven't one — at least, none that I want to part with."

"I'll bring it back," said Adye. "You'll be safe here."

Kemp gave him the weapon.

"Now for the door," said Adye.

As they stood waiting in the hall, they heard one of the bedroom windows crack. Kemp went to the door and began to turn the key as silently as he could. His face was a little paler than usual.

"You must step straight out," he said.

In another moment Adye was on the doorstep and the door was shut. He waited for a moment, feeling more comfortable with his back against the door. Then he marched down the steps. He crossed the grass and had almost reached the gate when something moved near him.

"Stop a bit," said a Voice, and Adye stopped, with his hand on the revolver.

"Well?" said Adye.

"Please go back to the house," said the Voice.

"No," said Adye. He thought of trying a shot in the direction of the Voice.

"What are you going to do?" said the Voice.

"What I do is my own business," said Adye.

The words were still on his lips when an arm came round his neck, he felt a knee in his back, and his head was forced backward. He fired the gun wildly, and in another moment he was struck in the mouth and the weapon was taken from his hand. He tried to struggle, and was thrown on his back.

"You devil!" said Adye.

The Voice laughed. "I would kill you now if it wasn't a waste of a shot," it said. Adye saw the revolver in the air, six feet off, pointing at him.

"Well?" said Adye, sitting up.

"Get up," said the Voice.

Adye stood up.

"Stand still," said the Voice, and then firmly. "Don't try any tricks. Remember I can see your face, if you can't see mine. You've got to go back to the house."

"He won't let me in," said Adye.

"That's a pity," said the Invisible Man. "It isn't you I want to kill."

Adye glanced away from the revolver and saw the sea far off, very blue and dark under the bright sun. He saw the smooth green hill, the white rocks of the coast, and the spreading town, and suddenly he knew that life was very sweet. His eyes came back to this little metal thing hanging between heaven and earth, six feet away. "What must I do?" he asked.

"What must *I* do?" asked the Invisible Man. "If I let you go, you'll get help. The only thing is for you to go back to the house."

"I'll try. If he lets me in, will you promise not to charge the door?"

"I don't want to fight *you*," said the Voice.

Kemp had hurried upstairs after letting Adye out, and now, looking through a broken window, he saw Adye stand talking with the unseen enemy. "Why doesn't he fire?" said Kemp to himself. Then the revolver moved a little.

"That's strange!" he said. "Adye has given up the revolver."

"Promise not to charge the door," Adye was saying. "Give me a chance."

"Just go back to the house. I tell you I'll promise nothing."

Adye seemed to decide suddenly. He turned towards the house, and walked slowly with his hands behind him. Kemp watched him. The revolver appeared, a small dark object, following Adye. Then things happened very quickly. Adye jumped at the small object, missed it, threw up his hands and fell forward on his face. A little ball of blue smoke rose into the air. Kemp did not hear the sound of the shot. Adye raised himself on one arm, fell forward, and lay still.

For a time Kemp remained looking at Adye as he lay peacefully on the grass. The day was very hot and still. Nothing seemed to move. Adye lay on the grass near the gate. The curtains of all the houses down the hill road were drawn, but in one little green garden hut was a white figure, rather like an old man asleep. Kemp's eyes returned to Adye — the game was not beginning well!

Then came a ringing and a knocking at the front door, but nobody opened it. Silence followed. Kemp sat listening and then began to look carefully out of the three windows, one after another. He went to the stairs and stood listening anxiously. What was his enemy doing?

Suddenly there was a banging from below. He waited and went down the stairs again. The house was filled with the sound of heavy blows and breaking wood. He went into the kitchen. The door was being broken down with an axe.

Kemp went back into the passage, trying to think. In a moment the Invisible Man would be in the kitchen. This door would not keep him a moment, and the——

The front-door bell rang again and Kemp heard voices. It was the policemen with the servant. He ran into the hall, opened the door, and three people fell into the house in a pile. Kemp shut the door again.

"The Invisible Man!" said Kemp. "He has a revolver — with two shots left. He's killed Adye. At least, he's shot him. Didn't you see him on the grass? He's lying there."

"Who?" said one of the policemen.

"Adye," said Kemp.

"We came round the back way," said the girl.

"What's that banging?" asked one of the policemen.

"He's in the kitchen — or will be. He's found an axe——"

Suddenly the house was full of the sound of the Invisible Man's blows on the kitchen door. The girl stared towards the kitchen and stepped into the dining room. Kemp tried to explain in broken sentences. They heard the kitchen door breaking open.

"This way," cried Kemp, and he pushed the policemen into the dining room doorway.

"The pokers," said Kemp, and rushed to the fire.

He handed a poker to each of the policemen.

He suddenly threw himself backwards. "Whup!" said one policeman, jumped to one side and caught the axe on his poker. The revolver cracked and shot a hole in a picture. The second policeman brought his poker down on the little weapon and sent it to the floor.

The axe went back into the passage. They could hear the Invisible Man breathing.

"Stand away, you two," he said. "I want that man Kemp."

"We want you," said the first policeman, taking a quick step forward and striking with his poker at the Voice. The Invisible Man must have stepped back and fallen over a chair.

Then, as the policeman went after him, the Invisible Man returned and struck him down.

But the second policeman, aiming behind the axe with his poker, hit something soft that cracked. There was a sharp cry of pain, and then the axe fell to the ground. The policeman struck again at emptiness and hit nothing; he put his foot on the axe and struck again. Then he stood, holding the poker, listening for the slightest movement.

He heard a window open, and a quick rush of feet outside. His companion rolled over and sat up, with blood running down between his eye and ear.

"Where is he?" asked the man on the floor.

"I don't know. I've hit him. He's standing somewhere in the hall unless he's slipped past you. Dr Kemp — sir!"

"Dr Kemp," cried the policeman again.

The second policeman began struggling to his feet. He stood up. Suddenly the faint sound of bare feet could be heard. "Whup!" cried the first policeman, and threw his poker.

He started to go after the Invisible Man. Then he changed his mind and stepped into the dining room.

"Dr Kemp——" he began.

The dining-room window was wide open, and neither servant nor Kemp was to be seen.

Chapter 22

The Hunter Hunted

Kemp had set off running, running to save his life as he had seen Mr Marvel run down the hill road. Never, he thought, had he seemed to run so slowly.

People looked at him. They saw fear in his face.

Now he was rushing to the town below, where people were standing or walking in groups.

He slowed down and then heard rapid footsteps behind.

"The Invisible Man," he cried. He thought of going into the police station, but changed his mind, turned down a side street and then into a yard, into a little house and so back into the main road.

A crowd had collected in the street; there was a noise of running feet. A big man, a few yards away, was swinging a heavy spade, striking at something. Another man came out of a shop with a thick stick in his hand. "Spread out! Spread out!" cried someone. Kemp stopped and looked round, breathing heavily. "He's close!" he cried. "Form a line across——"

He was hit hard under the ear and tried to turn round towards his unseen enemy. Then he was hit again under the jaw, and fell to the ground. In another moment a knee was digging into his chest and hands held his throat, but one hand was weaker than the other; then the spade of the big man came through the air above him, and struck something. He felt warm blood on his face. The hold on his throat was loosened and Kemp rolled on top of his enemy.

"I've got him!" cried Kemp. "Help! Help — hold him! He's down! Hold his feet!"

In another second there was a rush of people to the struggle. There was no shouting after Kemp's cry — only a sound of blows and feet and heavy breathing.

Then the Invisible Man got to his feet. Kemp still held his legs. Then someone got hold of his neck and pulled him back. Down went the pile of struggling, kicking men again. Then suddenly came a wild cry that died away into silence.

"Get back!" cried Kemp. "He's hurt, I tell you. Stand back."

A doctor was feeling the unseen body.

"The mouth is all wet," he said.

He stood up quickly, and then knelt down on the ground by the side of the unseen thing. More people joined the pushing crowd. Men were coming out of the houses. The doors of the inn stood wide open. Very little was said. Kemp felt around him; his hands seemed to pass through empty air. "He's not breathing," he said, and then, "I cannot feel his heart. His side — ugh!"

An old woman, looking under the arm of the big man with the spade, cried out. "Look there!" she said, and pointed. And looking where she pointed, everyone saw a shadowy, cloudy body. At first, they could see through it, but it was becoming more solid every moment.

"Hello!" cried the policeman. "Here are his feet showing!"

And so, slowly, beginning at his hands and feet, and spreading slowly to the centre of his body, that strange change continued. It was like the slow movement of a poison. They saw the glassy bones, then the flesh and skin, misty at first but slowly growing thicker and harder and more solid. Soon they could see his chest and his shoulders, and the faint shape of his face.

When at last the crowd made way for Kemp to stand back, there lay the bare and broken body of a young man of about thirty. His hair was white — not grey with age, but white as snow — and his eyes were bright like jewels. His expression was one of anger and fear.

"Cover his face!" cried a man. "In God's name, cover that face!"

Someone brought a sheet. They covered him, and carried him into the inn. And there it was, on a bed in an ill-lighted bedroom, among a crowd of excited people, that Griffin, the first of all men to make himself invisible, ended his strange and terrible life.

Word List

arrest (v) to take away, by law, someone who is thought to be a criminal

axe (n) a tool with a heavy metal blade on the end of a long handle, used to cut large pieces of wood

bandage (n/v) a long narrow piece of white cloth that is tied round a wound

bare (adj) not covered by clothes

bloodhound (n) a large dog with a very good sense of smell, often used for hunting

cabman (n) a man who drives a **carriage** which is hired like a taxi

carriage (n) a vehicle with wheels that is pulled by a horse

coach (n) a large **carriage** pulled by horses

Colonel (n) the title of someone who has achieved a high rank in the armed forces

cricket (n) a particular outdoor game in which players win points by hitting a ball and running

experiment (n/v) a test using scientific methods to discover how something reacts under certain conditions

fool (n) a stupid person or someone who has done something stupid

glove (n/v) something that you wear on your hand, usually with separate parts for each finger

greed (n) a strong desire for more money, power or possessions than you need

growl (v) to make the deep, angry sound that a dog makes in its throat

inn (n) a small hotel with a bar

jacket (n) a short coat

mad (adj) mentally ill; crazy

napkin (n) a small cloth used at meals for cleaning your mouth and hands

parlour (n) a room in a house used for receiving guests

poker (n) a metal stick used to move coal or wood in a fire to make it burn better

revolver (n) a small gun

scythe (n) a tool with a long, curved blade used for cutting long grass

shilling (n) a coin. In Britain there used to be twenty **shillings** to a pound.

sleeve (n) the part of a coat, shirt, etc. which covers your arm

sneeze (n/v) a sudden uncontrolled burst of air that comes from your nose, for example when you have a cold

stare (v) to look at someone or something for a long time without moving your eyes

tramp (n) a person with no home or job who wanders from place to place

vicar (n) a priest of the Church of England who is in charge of a church in a particular area. A **vicarage** is a house where a **vicar** lives.

visible (adj) that can be seen. Something that cannot be seen is **invisible**.

Activities

Chapters 1–4

Before you read

1 Look at the Word List on pages 72–3, and find words for:
 1 items of clothing.
 2 vehicles.
 3 buildings.
 4 money.
 5 tools.
 6 a weapon.
 7 jobs.
 8 a room.

2 What is an "invisible man"? Why do you think someone might want to become invisible?

After you read: Understanding

3 Are these statements about the Invisible Man true or false? Correct the false ones.
 1 He feels the cold.
 2 He eats and smokes.
 3 He enjoys the company of others.
 4 He has money.
 5 He gives Mrs Hall his name and address.
 6 He is a scientist.
 7 There is nothing under his clothes.

4 Who are:
 1 Mr and Mrs Hall?
 2 Millie?
 3 Teddy Henfrey?
 4 Fearenside?
 5 Cuss?
 6 Bunting?

After you read: Speaking

5   Work in pairs. Imagine a conversation between Mrs Hall and Cuss.
     Student A: You are Mrs Hall. Describe the Invisible Man's appearance on his
     arrival at the inn, and say how you felt about him.
     Student B: You are Cuss. Explain why you decided to talk to the stranger,
     what happened and how you felt.
     Then, still playing these parts, discuss possible explanations for this strange
     figure.

Chapters 5–8

Before you read

6   Look at the titles of the next few chapters. What do you think the answers are
     to the questions?
     The Robbery at the Vicarage
     1   Who is the thief?
     2   What does he steal?
     The Furniture That Went Mad
     3   How does furniture "go mad"?
     The Stranger Shows His Face
     4   Who does he show it to?
     5   What does it look like?
     On the Road
     6   Why does the stranger leave the inn?

After you read: Understanding

7   As you read, find the answers to the questions in Activity 6.

8 Why:
1 do the Buntings wait until the servant is in the kitchen before they go upstairs?
2 do the Halls hear coughs and sneezes on their stairs?
3 does Mrs Hall stop answering the stranger's bell?
4 does the stranger's nose roll across the floor?
5 does he take his shirt off?
6 does Jaffers lie on the ground without moving?
7 does the Invisible Man throw stones at the tramp?
8 does the tramp try to enter the parlour at the inn?

After you read: Speaking

9 Explain how:
1 Mr and Mrs Bunting are robbed.
2 the Halls know that the stranger left the inn during the night.
3 the stranger removes Mrs Hall from his bedroom.
4 the stranger escapes from the policeman and the crowd of villagers.

Chapters 9–13

Before you read

10 How do you think Mr Marvel managed to take the clothes and books from the inn?

After you read: Understanding

11 Who is talking to whom? Who or what are they talking about?
1 ". . . it's all Greek or Russian or some other language."
2 "He's got my trousers — and all the vicar's clothes!"
3 "I've got a weak heart."
4 "There isn't any Invisible Man at all."
5 "He seems to be in a hurry."

12 What is "the story of the flying money"?

After you read: Speaking

13 Discuss the development of the Invisible Man's character and attitudes. What was he like when he arrived at the inn? What is he like now? How do you think he will change as the story continues?

Chapters 14–17

Before you read

14 Give your opinion.
 1 Will Mr Marvel escape from the Invisible Man?
 2 How will Dr Kemp become important to the story?
 3 Is there any way of catching someone who is invisible?

After you read: Understanding

15 Use one word to complete these sentences.
 1 Mr Marvel is .... of the Invisible Man.
 2 The man with the black beard's solution is to .... the Invisible Man.
 3 Dr Kemp shares a house with his ....
 4 A spot of .... is the first evidence of the Invisible Man's presence in Kemp's house.
 5 Dr Kemp finds it .... to believe that a man can be invisible.
 6 He believes that Griffin should be ....
 7 As a science student, Griffin was interested in ....
 8 His father .... himself because he owed the money that Griffin had stolen from him.
 9 Before Griffin left his room in London, he set .... to the house.

The Invisible Man

After you read: Speaking

16 Work in pairs and act out the conversation between Dr Kemp and Griffin, using your own words.
Student A: You are Dr Kemp. Ask questions to find out how and why Griffin became invisible.
Student B: Answer Dr Kemp's questions by telling the story of your scientific experiments.

Chapters 18–22

Before you read

17 What has driven Griffin to behave as he does? How far do you think he is prepared to go to achieve his aims?

After you read: Understanding

18 Answer these questions about the story.
1 What did Griffin plan to do in Port Burdock?
2 What does he tell Kemp is his plan now?
3 What does Kemp plan to do when Adye and his men arrive?
4 Why does his plan fail?
5 What happens to Mr Wicksteed?
6 Who is the next person to be wounded or killed?
7 Who catches Griffin?
8 What happens to Griffin as he dies?

After you read: Speaking

19 Discuss the measures that Kemp explains to Colonel Adye are necessary to catch Griffin. How helpful is his advice?

Whole book

Writing

1   What kind of man is Griffin? Describe his character.

2   Imagine you are Kemp. Write a letter to a college friend who also knew Griffin. Tell him/her about your recent experiences.

3   Choose a character other than Griffin and Kemp and explain the part he/she plays in the story.

4   Imagine that you could make yourself invisible. How would you use this ability?

5   The writer appears to be making a connection between scientific discovery and power. What possible connections can there be? Give other true examples of the way scientific discoveries have been used to harm or control others.

6   Write a book report for someone who is considering reading *The Invisible Man*. Without spoiling the story by telling too much of it, explain why you did or did not enjoy it.